GRAY GHOST

(Bill Dix Detective Series)

By

C.L. Swinney

GRAY GHOST

(Bill Dix Detective Series)

By

C.L. Swinney

Published By:
RJ Parker Publishing, Inc.

ISBN-13: 978-1503167667
ISBN-10: 1503167666

GRAY GHOST

Copyright © 2015
by C.L.Swinney

United States of America

License Notes

This book is licensed for your personal enjoyment only. This book may not be resold or given away to other people. Please respect the author's work. All rights reserved. No parts of this publication can be reproduced or transmitted in any form or by any means without prior written authorization from Chris Swinney.

This book is a work of fiction

The unauthorized reproduction or distribution of a copyrighted work is illegal. Criminal copyright infringement, including infringement without monetary gain, is investigated by the FBI and is punishable by fines and federal imprisonment.

Dedication

This book is for my parents who instilled in me strong values and determination, my wife and two sons for their tremendous support, my friends, and the law enforcement community. I truly appreciate all of your support. And for the boys in blue—past, current, and future—thank you for risking your lives every day to keep the world a better place.

About the Author

C. L. Swinney is a narcotics investigator in the San Francisco Bay area. He's investigated hundreds of narcotics, homicide, gang, and Mexico cartel cases along the west coast of the United States, Mexico, and Canada. He's been invited to speak at law enforcement conferences throughout the United States and is recognized as an expert in narcotics, homicides, and cell phone forensics. The world of narcotics is dark and mysterious. C.L. Swinney will grab your imagination and keep you guessing in his fascinating debut novel.

Acknowledgements

I'd like to thank author Sunny Frazier for giving me a shot in the writing business, and all my writing pals who have helped me through this process: the Coast Guard members I interviewed tirelessly for this project, members of law enforcement in Miami and California, my co-workers, DMV staff, Stafford Creek Lodge, Leland Flyfishing Outfitters, and last but not least, I'd like to thank God for keeping me on the right path.

CHAPTER ONE

Moments before dawn and half a mile offshore of the Caribbean island of Andros, Sean heard something smash into the rear of the speedboat and disintegrate the motors.

"Pres, get your gun ready. Someone wants the load." Sean quickly chambered a round in his AK-47. He brushed away shrapnel from the fragmented engine case at his feet and scanned for the shooter, or shooters.

Since they'd operated without navigational equipment or lights, and used muffled motors, Sean believed his speedboat, *Gray Ghost*, was nearly invisible. But, somebody on the island had fired at them.

"Preston!" Sean shouted. He briefly turned on his flashlight to see why his brother hadn't answered. The light fell on a long piece of metal embedded in Preston's forehead. His body still twitched, but he was obviously dead.

Sean screamed as the gruesome sight registered in his brain and instinctively tried to duck for cover just as another round nearly decapitated him.

Gray Ghost sank to the ocean floor, along with one hundred million dollars' worth of cocaine, tucked away in her hull.

* * * *

The hired sniper had painstakingly scoped out the area earlier and knew the two houses on the north end of the island were occupied. Lights went on as the blasts rang through the night. This had not been part of the plan because he knew there was no way to retrieve the boat at night. His specialty was rifles, not underwater retrieval. *Son-of-a- bitch.*

He realized he'd have to advise the man he knew simply as "the Caller." More importantly, the gunman needed to remain concealed long enough to secure the speedboat.

* * * *

The Caller was aware of his hired man's mistake. His contingency plan was already initiated. Retrieving the contents of the speedboat, sunk or not, would happen. The hundred million dollar payday, and the Caller's ability to walk away from the business for good depended on it.

CHAPTER TWO

A small single-engine prop Cessna swayed on approach to the Mangrove Cay Airport, in the Bahamas. In the last row, a large man with long hair and goatee glanced at his seatmate. "Christ, Dix, you think this tin can's gonna make it?"

"Oh yeah. It'll hold together," Dix said calmly. "These Cessna Skyhawks can take a lot of abuse. Just relax. We'll be on the ground pretty quick."

"You sure? We're tossing around like a ping pong ball up here."

"C'mon, Petersen. We've been through worse things than this," Dix replied. "Just think about seven days of fishing and six nights of relaxing in that classy resort."

Petersen shrugged, trying to shake out his tense shoulders.

"Man. I'm ready for that. We're certainly due for a break, buddy."

Dix thought a moment. "Yup... change of scene, leave Miami behind. No drug dealers, no chasing bad guys, just fresh air and sunshine."

Petersen was beginning to think this trip might not have been worth six years' overtime... and a divorce. *The narcotics world is dirty all the way around.*

Dix felt the airspeed decrease as the small plane started to descend from turbulent airspace.

Petersen looked out his window. He noticed scattered freshwater lakes surrounded by green trees and brush. He'd read online that these were known as "blue holes," and were well known by divers. He motioned out the window to Dix, who turned to his window and looked back with a smile.

The pilot brought the plane down safely with a bumpy landing on a pothole-littered runway.

Petersen noticed the remnants of five or six single-engine planes in the dogwood bushes and Spanish stopper trees bordering the tiny airstrip. Pigeon plum and snake bark limbs grew through older carcasses of similar planes. Native palms and a rinky-dink chain link fence surrounded the airport.

After regaining his composure and releasing his grip on the armrests, he found his voice. "You think those birds were used for smuggling dope?"

Dix glanced out the window and casually replied, "I'd say so. One appears to have crashed recently."

"What makes you think that?"

"The other planes have been stripped down almost completely. Seats, doors, wheels, anything that could be removed with small tools is gone. I suspect the contents of the planes, probably narcotics, were the first to go. Then the parts were salvaged as spares."

Petersen figured all the plane hardware was worth a lot. "Petersen," Dix said, "You've been involved in little league games for way too long. You haven't worked a decent drug bust in at least two years. You've lost your edge buddy. Focus and maybe you'll make sergeant someday." He grinned.

Petersen replied with a single finger gesture. Then he responded, "I simply chose family over the office." This was mostly true. He'd always put his family first, and the decision had cost him professionally.

"Then why'd Angie shack up with that rookie hotshot from the Navy?" Dix asked. His expression indicated he regretted having brought up the painful subject.

Petersen blamed their profession. He knew all too well the twisted sense of humor cops developed to cope with the situations they were exposed to. Relationships took a backseat to the hectic, stressful life of narcotics investigation. Still, they were close friends, and Dix shouldn't have gone there.

"Sorry, Steve, that was out of line." Dix looked remorseful.

Petersen didn't answer.

Dix continued, "As soon as we get back, I'll arrange for the little bastard to meet some friends of mine, you know, semi-retired special ops pals. I'm pretty sure they can convince him to leave married women alone."

Although Petersen would have loved to see the man who stole his wife get pummeled, he realized only he, Angie, Dix, and the Navy hotshot would ever know exactly how the incident went down. But Petersen knew it wasn't entirely the guy's fault. "That won't be necessary, Bill, she made her choice. He obliged."

Two days after Petersen's life had been shattered, he learned from Dix the rookie seamen had completed paperwork requesting an Immediate transfer to Alaska. The request stated the bastard didn't feel comfortable staying in Miami.

Dix suddenly asked, "You brought the Crazy Charlies and Borski Epoxy Back Shrimp, right?"

Petersen was grateful for the change of subject. "I most certainly did, but only enough for me. You're on your own, asshole."

Dix raised his right eyebrow. "No problem, I figured you'd say that, so I picked up a few dozen from the fly shop yesterday morning, even a few new patterns. And I don't intend to share, either.

The gray-haired pilot unbuckled, squeezed out of his seat, turned to his passengers, and smiled. "Well, that was close. It's a good thing I kept both eyes open on the final approach." Then he motioned to the door. "Let's see what's happening on the island."

Petersen noticed a sand-colored minivan parked near the tarmac. It looked rusty underneath, covered with debris, and in need of a wash. However, the tires appeared new.

Steve Petersen could hear the engine idling smoothly and noticed it was unoccupied.

"Turtle Cay Lodge" was painted in rainbow colors on the side. A tall man who looked like a local, with an athletic build, dressed in a brilliantly colored print shirt and khakis, held a sign that read, "Mr. Dix and Mr. Petersen."

The weather seemed perfect. A slight breeze blew off the ocean while a few bright white clouds drifted high in the beautiful blue sky and looked like a screen saver. The thermometer by the luggage carousel read eighty-one degrees Fahrenheit, but the breeze made it feel more like seventy-eight.

Petersen noticed the small, single lane road adjacent to the airport was the only way in or out. It was guarded by two Royal Bahamian police officers who were heavily armed. An older model Jeep

Wrangler carrying three more officers sped by them headed in the direction of the tarmac.

The detectives climbed into the weathered minivan.

Petersen said, "Looks like someone might be headed for a bad day." He watched the Jeep go straight, make a hard right, and motor directly toward the downed plane Dix had noticed earlier. He guessed the plane had gone down not long before their arrival, and, as Dix had surmised, no one had had an opportunity to pillage it yet because it was still daylight.

"Those boys are going to have a field day with that one," Dix said.

Almost immediately after the Bahamian officers exited the vehicle and surveyed the airplane, two of the men gave each other high fives. The third man, who seemed to be in charge, said something to them. Dix had noticed the guy's confident way of carrying himself. Both men stopped their small celebration and began their inspection.

The movement caught the attention of the van driver. He made eye contact with someone in the direction of the downed plane who returned a subtle movement with his head and neck. Dix and Petersen were pushed back into their seats as the force of the driver stepping on the accelerator caught them off guard. They exchanged glances.

"I don't give a damn what's happening." Dix straightened in his seat. "I just want to get to Turtle Cay Lodge in one piece."

Petersen nodded his agreement as the van roared out onto the main road.

CHAPTER THREE

The Turtle Cay Lodge was nestled among native palms, just footsteps from the clear, calm waters of Elliott Creek. The brochure had insisted prehistoric tarpon could be enticed to inhale a well-placed cockroach fly right from the dock in front of the lodge.

According to what Dix had read on the website, previous guests reported the food was terrific, the service was impeccable, and the fly fishing was spectacular. The place had opened in 1995 and barely made enough money to pay the bills the first season. Now, seventeen years later, the lodge had a long waiting list of folks anxious to experience what the advertising called, "Heaven on Earth." In fact, if it weren't for Dix's connections, Petersen would have had to wait two more years to get this dream shot at a trophy bonefish on a fly tied by his own hand.

Dix guessed the Bahamian people usually enjoyed life to the fullest. However, his detective intuition and the scene at the airport told him something wasn't quite right. As the minivan finally slowed and they came to a stop along Elliot Creek, the driver turned and grinned. "Welcome to the finest lodge in the Bahamas, mon."

The main lodge and adjacent cottages looked recently remodeled. They had tiled roofs and were surrounded by Bahamian pine trees and thatch palms. Flagstone paths led to the main lodge, the cottages, and out toward the water.

"Is there always this much police activity on the island?" Dix asked.

The driver didn't respond, so he continued, "We saw quite a few officers, and they all seemed to be in a hurry."

"Well, mon, you came a long way and spent a bunch of money to catch da bonefish, tarpon, and permit. Island politics shouldn't spoil your vacation."

Dix raised an eyebrow. "We're interested. Why don't you try us?" He never got his answer because another man and woman approached.

"Oh look, here comes Martin, the owner of this grand place."

The couple came to the side of the van, and the man they assumed was Martin looked grim and seemed preoccupied. Dix thought it was strange because he figured the amount of money he and Petersen had paid should have kept the guy quite happy.

"Gentlemen, welcome to Turtle Cay Lodge. It's a pleasure to have you here." His cell phone rang. "Business call. Please make yourselves at home." He motioned to the small thatched buildings along the south side of the lodge while he answered the phone and walked away.

Dix looked at the cottages and noticed air conditioning units protruding from the windows and hammocks swaying between palms.

The woman smiled and extended her hand to Petersen. "Hello, I'm Suzanne Hamilton, but you can call me Suzie. My husband's name is Martin." She gestured toward the man who'd greeted them moments earlier.

Dix shook her hand and couldn't hide his sheepish grin. "Mrs. Hamilton, it is a pleasure to see you again. You're even prettier than when I saw you last."

She giggled and blushed slightly. Then she embraced him. "Bill, you always knew how to charm the ladies."

Dix turned to Petersen. "I guess I forgot to tell you. Steve, meet my college sweetheart, Suzie." Before long, Dix regaled his partner with the story of how they'd met. He and Suzie reminisced about their university days.

Petersen listened and smiled and laughed at the appropriate time.

After a few minutes, Dix grinned. "How else did you think we were able to get a spot at the lodge two years sooner than the established waiting list?"

Petersen laughed. "Whatever you had to do to get us here was well worth it."

"It was nothing." Dix winked at Suzie. "I just had to make a few phone calls and pull a few strings."

Suzie said playfully, "Don't let him fool you, Steve. I owed him big time for helping my aunt who lives in Miami."

Dix thought to himself. *Looks like she's trying to appear happy. I know her well enough to sense something's bothering her. If the bastard isn't treating her right, I'll kill him.*

Just then, the monstrous silver back of a fish with a black dorsal fin emerged out of the water about thirty yards off the main dock. It looked like a mini-submarine. Dix had never seen anything like it before. They all stopped talking and the men both said in unison, "What is that?"

Suzie smiled, "Oh, that. It's an adult tarpon, probably around two hundred pounds."

Dix and Petersen looked at each other, astounded.

Suzie laughed. "You might even catch one. As long as we can find two more guides."

With that, Suzie showed the detectives to their cottage and told them the meal schedule. She pointed out the mini refrigerators, fully stocked with beer.

"Perfect." Dix hugged her again before she left.

Dix walked around the room looking in drawers and flipping switches to see what they did. The bathroom had marble flooring and a walk-in shower. He noticed there was no television or telephone. Two double beds, each covered with colorful island print spreads, seemed cozy with oak frames and white canopies overhead. Despite being small, the room felt classy and comfortable.

After showering, putting on clean clothes, and powering down three Red Stripe beers each, the room-to-room intercom system buzzed. Dix pushed the button.

A voice with a decidedly Caribbean accent announced, "Your presence is requested at the main house for dinner with the Hamiltons."

They'd expected to eat in the huge kitchen and dining area with the other guests, so the invitation came as a surprise.

As they walked over to the main house, Dix asked, "Why do you think our guides aren't available. Maybe they're sick."

Petersen grinned. "Maybe they were murdered."

Dix shook his head. "No shop talk. They're probably just sick."

The guys arrived in the private dining room to find Martin, dressed in a neatly pressed print shirt, khaki shorts, and flip-flops. He waited for them at a massive oak table, looking relaxed and slightly intoxicated.

Martin smiled. "Well, you want the good news or the bad?"

Dix spoke first. "I like to hear bad news first. It makes the good news, even when it isn't that great, seem better."

"And I like the good news first. That way the bad news doesn't seem so bad," said Petersen.

"How about I tell them?" Suzie suggested as she joined them. She looked stunning in a long, light green floral-print dress. But her eyes appeared to be red and puffy as though she'd been crying.

Dix clenched his jaw. *Martin better not have put a hand on her or I'm going to personally kick the crap out of him.*

Martin looked at this wife. "No. I'll do it. My closest friends, and the best two guides on Andros Island, Sean and Preston Smith, were found dead just offshore this morning. They'd been missing for three days. Suzie and I were questioned at length by Superintendent Charles Taylor from the Royal Bahamian Police Department." Suzie began to cry and Martin put his arm around her as tears ran down his own cheeks.

Their pain was hard to watch, especially since Dix and Petersen had lost far too many close friends and knew the terrible feeling that came with it.

"Martin, I am sorry for your loss," Dix said. "We had no idea. Otherwise, we'd have canceled the trip." His beer buzz disappeared immediately.

Suzie sniffled. "It's okay guys. You couldn't have known about any of this. It happened so suddenly. We know how much this trip means to you, and we want you to have a fantastic time. Martin has been trying to replace your guides since you arrived."

Of all the dumb luck. Dix had been amazed by the beauty of the island and was captivated by the atmosphere of the lodge. Now he felt like he was plunked in the middle of another criminal investigation. He wanted to help Suzie. It really bothered him to see her suffer.

Petersen spoke for both of them. "Mr. and Mrs. Hamilton, we can come back here another time. Maybe things need to calm down a bit."

Martin replied, "Nonsense. Sean and Preston would have wanted you two to experience this opportunity in their honor. I have secured the services of two well-qualified Bahamian guides for you." He'd stopped crying and seemed more in control of his emotions. Suzie still wept quietly.

"Fellas." Dix motioned to the outside. "I've lost my appetite. Let's go out for some fresh air." He patted his chest pocket. "Maybe we can see if these authentic Cohibas were worth fifteen dollars each."

Shortly after they left the main house, Dix noticed a red Subaru station wagon speeding toward the lodge. It was occupied by two men. The vehicle leaned heavily to the right, almost hitting the ground on the passenger side, and it had some minor front end damage.

As the car passed, Dix saw it was also missing a rear bumper. In Miami, this type of vehicle screamed, "Please pull me over." In the Bahamas, it was known as a "work vehicle."

The Subaru skidded to a stop a few feet beyond where they stood, and the driver quickly exited. He was handsome, probably in his forties, with a dark complexion, about Petersen's height, but leaner. He immediately approached the men.

"Hello, mon. My name is Wilfred Jones. It's a pleasure to meet you." He spoke with a subtle British accent.

Dix and Petersen shook Wilfred's hand.

Their attention was drawn back to the vehicle. The distinctive tilt had Dix curious about the person who occupied the passenger seat.

A loud creaking noise emanated from the beat-up car as the door swung open. One leg emerged, and the whole vehicle began to clank and bang. As the man stepped out, Dix could almost hear the car whisper, "Thank you." Dix figured the guy was about six feet six inches tall, with a muscular build, probably weighed over 250 pounds. He seemed to be a local, and bore a faint resemblance to Wilfred.

"Wow!" exclaimed Petersen.

"I hope this guy's a friend of Wilfred's," said Dix.

The passenger slowly and deliberately walked over to them, said something to Wilfred neither American could understand. He spoke in the thick British dialect of the island. Then the new arrival extended his massive hand to Petersen.

"Nice to meet you, sir. My name is Bobby Jones, but you can call me Bubba."

Bubba shook Petersen's hand, and then Dix's. Dix wondered if he'd ever regain feeling after the vise-like shake.

Martin said, "Gentlemen, these are two more of my friends. They're experienced fishing guides. I have asked them to take you on the world's greatest saltwater fly fishing adventure. They've guided for me as side work from time to time over the years."

Dix reached into his pocket and offered each of them a cigar, which they both accepted. As they lighted up, Dix asked, "Which species of fish do you think is the most difficult to catch?"

They answered in unison, "Permit, mon."

Dix smiled. "Then let's go after them last. How about it, Petersen?"

"Let me finish this cigar and see if Martin has some whiskey. Then I'll agree." The Jones brothers and the detectives discussed arrangements for the next day's trip while they puffed away.

"We'll pick you up at the lodge dock at eight in the morning," said Will. "Bubba and I will take you to Fresh Creek first, then explore the rest of the east side of Andros."

Dix and Petersen shared a grin. "That sounds awesome," replied Petersen.

Martin returned with glasses of whiskey, and the men sat on the dock overlooking Elliott Creek, watching the sun dance on the ripples.

After they finished their cigars and said their goodbyes, Dix headed back to the cottage to discover his friend swinging in a hammock.

Dix obviously startled Petersen with his approach. "Hey man, you shouldn't have smoked that cigar. You know those things make you sick."

"I know. But I haven't had one in so long. I figured I could treat myself."

Dix noticed his friend looked somber and a bit shaken up. "You okay, buddy?"

Petersen didn't answer right away. He gazed out toward Elliot Creek and shook his head. "I can't get my mind off my ex. It's terrible what she did, but I miss her."

Dix nodded and knew he needed to tread lightly here. "That's totally normal, Steve. No matter what happens down the road, I've got your back. Now, let's hit the sack so you can sleep off that Cuban and we can get some rest for a kick ass day of fishing tomorrow."

Petersen stared at Dix and replied, "I know buddy, I know. Thank you."

Dix walked his friend to their cottage. They discussed how eager they were to go fishing, but each secretly wondered what happened to their original guides.

No matter where I go, I seem to get into some sort of mess, thought Dix.

CHAPTER FOUR

At seven forty-five, Dix shook Petersen until he woke up.

Petersen felt sick, and his head was pounding. Every second or so, Petersen felt his heartbeat at the center of his brain. He realized the glass of whiskey hadn't done him in. It was the damn cigar.

"Man, take it easy on me. I feel like throwing up."

Dix chuckled. "I warned you about the cigar. Now hurry and get up. I took our gear and food to the dock already."

"Okay, okay, but could you stop yelling?" Petersen popped several aspirin and drank two bottles of water to try to accelerate the healing process. He threw on a flats fishing shirt, grabbed his hat and sunglasses, and followed Dix to the dock.

Two idling Maverick flats fishing boats waited for them at the dock. Petersen grabbed his head and gave Dix a *God help me* look.

"Don't look at me, buddy. I thought maybe you'd learned your lesson about smoking cigars from the last trip. I guess not."

Bubba stood next to the larger boat. He was wearing khaki pants, a long sleeve shirt and had an obviously too small, large-brimmed hat perched on his head. His shadow nearly covered the dock.

Wilfred stood with one foot on the dock and one on the smaller boat, motioning for Dix and Petersen to hurry. Dix noticed he wore the same clothes from the night before.

Dix whistled. He loved boats. "Man, is that a Maverick?"

"Sure is," replied Wilfred.

"What kind of engine does she have? It looks huge."

"It's a four stroke Yamaha. Two hundred horsepower. Just came out last year. She gets up and goes," said Wilfred.

Dix was impressed. He couldn't wait to head out and see what the boat could do at top speed.

"Now don't be bashful, Mr. Dix. Bubba promised to take it easy on you," said Wilfred.

"That's reassuring," said Dix as he boarded the boat. "That leaves the drunken sailor with me." Wilfred motioned for Petersen to board his boat.

All he was able to muster was, "Okay."

Bubba grinned. "Mon, you're a wreck. Let's go look for some fish." Dix shot Petersen a look of concern.

"I'll be okay." Petersen was lying, but he didn't want any of the guys to give him crap about not being able to handle a glass of whiskey and a single cigar.

The flats boats began the hour-long journey through Elliott Creek to Joulters Cays in the search of trophy fish. Due to their design, the boats could easily maneuver over the emerald green, shallow water on the myriad of flats in the area. Yet, they were sturdy enough to take on some chop from the deep, blue Atlantic Ocean.

As soon as Wilfred guided the boat into the open water of the Atlantic Ocean, Petersen promptly vomited. *That's much better.*

* * * *

Dix enjoyed the trip out to the fishing grounds. He saw small, colorful homes dotting the island and watched as a large stingray jumped out of the water near his boat. The trees and bushes seemed brilliantly green and the various island birds stalked the water along the shore looking for prey. The maze of shallow flats, intertwined by channels and into the open sea, looked like a jigsaw puzzle. Occasionally, Dix smelled cooked food in the air when the island jutted out closer to the channels. His stomach growled. When he envisioned Andros Island back in Miami, he couldn't recall it being this amazing.

Bubba pulled the power back on the engine and the boat coasted onto a large flat. Dix thought he saw a sea turtle and was impressed with the abundance of wildlife and sea creatures in the area.

When Bubba grabbed his push pole from the inside railing of the boat, he labored to get up on the poling platform. Dix walked to the bow of the boat. He tied on a fly pattern that looked like a shrimp and worked out some line from his reel. His pulse accelerated, and he stared at the water hoping to see movement below the surface.

Bubba surveyed the water above the flat. "Should be some bonefish here, mon. Dey use dey noses to rustle out crabs and shrimp. Then dey tails stick out of the water 'cause the depth's shallow on the flats. Dis is called tailing." Bubba scanned the water intently. Then he pointed to three tails about thirty feet away.

He turned to Dix and whispered, "Get ready. They at twelve o'clock, moving right to left."

Bubba slowly and quietly pushed the flatboat closer to the feeding fish. "Okay, get the fly right in front dey noses." Dix whipped the rod back and forth and worked out some line. He placed the fly about three feet in front of the fish and was shocked he'd done such a perfect cast on the first try.

"Strip the fly. Okay, stop. Now, do it again."

Dix moved the fly, and the lead bonefish inhaled it and took off in the opposite direction so fast Dix barely had time to react. The line pulled through the rod guides quickly as the fish tried to seek refuge in nearby mangroves. Dix set the hook and began fighting. After a few minutes, he brought his tiring prey close to the boat. Bubba retrieved it, and they gave each other high-fives.

Bubba laughed. "You can breathe now, buddy."

Dix hadn't felt excitement like that when fighting and catching fish in a long time. It reminded him of his younger days on patrol while chasing bad guys on foot. "Bubba, that was awesome," he exclaimed.

Something had caught Bubba's attention and Bill turned to see what it was. It looked like a red and white Coast Guard cutter, a helicopter, and a smaller gray boat. They seemed to be combing the water southwest of their location.

"What the hell are those guys up to?" he wondered aloud.

"Dey been out there since yesterday after dey found Sean."

Dix heard a motor coming from behind him. He turned around to see Wilfred and Petersen heading toward him.

Wilfred coasted his boat to a stop near them. The two boats were within earshot of each other.

Dix became more alert as his mind began to wonder about what really was happening on the island. He figured someone had dedicated a lot of resources to the search. *Knock it off. You're on vacation.* But his detective's curiosity won out. "Could I ask you a few questions? You know, in an effort to figure out what exactly happened the other day." Dix tried to sound casual, but the excitement of the day and of the possibility of danger probably came through.

A large helicopter flew toward them, and eventually directly overhead. The blade wash rippled the water, and the sound was deafening. It continued toward the open ocean. *What are they looking for?*

Bubba appeared thoughtful for several minutes but didn't say a word.

Finally, Wilfred said, "We heard some *sip-sip*." Seeing Dix and Petersen's confusion, he chuckled. "That's Bahamian for gossip. But you can't trust the island talk."

Dix knew their guides weren't aware his offer came from one of the top murder and narcotic detectives in Florida. He smiled. "Guys, I've had a lot of experience in this kind of thing. You want help, just let me know."

Bubba rubbed his chin.

Dix was confused. "I can help." Bubba did not respond.

Finally Bubba said, "Maybe dey looking for the boat."

"Were Preston and Sean on a boat recently? Before their bodies were found?"

Bubba clammed up again.

"Only reason someone would look for a boat would be if the authorities thought your friends were on one when they were killed," said Dix. "Or they got a tip they were in a boat, but there's something on it... or in it."

Bubba's eyes flickered indicating to Dix he was on to something.

"Yup. Preston and Sean were in a boat. And, we heard there might be lots of cocaine in it."

"Really? Who told you that?" "Just word on da street."

"But do you think it's true?" Dix was now excited. If the boat held cocaine, a great deal of what he'd observed since he arrived made more sense.

Bubba looked away. Dix had interrogated some great criminal minds in his career. He was excellent at extracting information. Bubba's reaction indicated he had more to say. "Look, let's just catch some fish. If you want to talk, I'm all ears."

Petersen shot his partner a quick glance and shrugged.

Bubba didn't reply. He fired up the engine, and they headed for the next fishing flat, followed by Wilfred and Petersen.

For the next four hours, the boats stayed relatively close to one another, so Dix and Petersen could watch as they each hooked and fought a fish. Dix would have preferred to be in a single boat. However, casting in fly fishing required ample room behind the fisherman. Most people fished the flats with a guide and single fisherman on each boat to avoid hooking themselves while casting.

At one point, Dix stopped to admire Petersen's effortless and majestic casting stroke. He'd stopped fishing completely and watched Petersen with great interest. A few minutes later, Petersen and Wilfred grew very still. Dix wondered what was going on when he noticed Wilfred pointing at the water. *Ah hah.*

A few seconds later, Petersen set the hook and a wily bonefish ripped off the flat, looking for salvation in deeper waters. *Man, this is gonna be the best vacation ever*, he thought.

* * * *

Wilfred jumped down from the poling platform, located at the rear of the boat above the engine and secured the push pole in the railing mount to move to another flat. Petersen noticed the Coast Guard circus had cleared. Wilfred fired up the four-stroke Yamaha engine and headed directly to where the boats and the helicopter had been. Wilfred had a gut feeling *Gray Ghost* would be far south of where the Coast Guard had looked.

As a long time fishing guide and resident of the island, Wilfred knew the water very well. He was obligated to take his client to the best spot to catch fish, but he was also interested in the sunken boat. Knowing the local sip-sip often held elements of the truth, he pointed to the right. "We'll start right over there. That's where they think Sean and Preston's bodies came from, based on the currents in the area. I don't really want to go where my friends were murdered, but I also wish to pay my last respects. Besides, it's a good place to catch fish."

"Given the time, wind patterns, and ocean currents, it seems highly unlikely there's anything remaining from the incident." Petersen stared ahead.

"Light things, like clothes and life vests, would be gone. But the boat would remain if it's in shallow water, especially a thirty-seven-foot speedboat loaded with 1,250 kilos of cocaine." Wilfred looked at Petersen for a reaction. He got none.

Petersen cautiously eyed Wilfred. Large amounts of narcotics didn't impress him, he'd seen his share. However, he began to wonder just how much these guides knew about what had happened to their friends. Wilfred had told him an exact weight of cocaine suspected to be in the speedboat. *Was this the sip-sip Wilfred had mentioned? Wait. I'm supposed to be on vacation.*

"How do you know?" His training took over.

"It's too much weight and the current is slow here. The boat and the cocaine will be intact."

"No, how do you know there are 1250 kilos in the boat?"

Wilfred chuckled. "It's what I heard." Petersen remained cautious.

The guide gave the engine full throttle and the boat planed and took off.

Ten minutes later, Wilfred cut the power to the engine. He had been quiet for the entire ride. Wilfred retrieved his push-pole and climbed up to the guide platform. Slowly, he pushed the boat along the grass-covered flat. The water was clear and appeared to be about three feet deep.

He seemed to be looking for fish when he pointed to a film on the surface, about forty feet to the left. Immediately, checking his boat engine to see if it was leaking, he said, "Nothing's coming from here." He became visibly excited and slowly used his pole to move the boat closer to the slick.

When they were near, he jumped down from the guide tower and checked the depth finder.

Petersen watched him with a great deal of interest. He realized he was out of his element and all alone with a fishing guide who had too much knowledge of the situation. He watched Wilfred's hands intently. *You never know...*

Steve decided to try to figure out what Wilfred knew. "Wilfred, why didn't you just tell me you were looking for Sean and Preston's boat?"

He seemed to hesitate, then looked at Petersen. "Why, you want to help?"

"Absolutely." Petersen looked at the depth finder to get a reading while Wilfred opened the compartment at the bow of the boat. As a recreational diver, Petersen recognized diving equipment carefully stashed inside. He saw fins, two air tanks, weight belts, and a rope. Wilfred grinned and donned the diving gear.

What they saw on the fish finder indicated they were directly over something large. The film on the water suggested the object was leaking fuel and oil. Whatever it was, it sat on the ocean floor at roughly twenty-five feet below the surface.

Petersen heard another boat engine and looked up to see Bubba and Dix slowing down to fish about a quarter mile away.

Just north of the object on the fish finder screen, the ocean floor plummeted to several hundred feet and eventually several thousand. Petersen was pretty sure Wilfred wouldn't have much time to examine whatever was below them based on the depth, strong currents, and minimal air in the small oxygen tanks. Plus, they had no idea if it was *Gray Ghost*.

Petersen recalled the concern their friends felt for the dead men. Even though he'd never met them, he felt like he wanted to help bring closure to their families. This feeling had drawn him to law enforcement in the first place. He genuinely liked helping people.

Wilfred began to feed Petersen more information. "I'm pretty sure Sean and Preston were running dope. Bubba and I think they were killed while transporting the stuff to Miami."

Petersen thought it funny how people always told him everything without much effort on his part. He'd been successful at his job because he was a good listener. He decided his initial assessment that Wilfred might be a threat was wrong. *This is shaping up to be a real mystery.*

After he had finished talking, Wilfred entered the water.

Petersen kept the boat steady with the anchor and monitored the rope they'd tied onto Wilfred for safety. It seemed as if Wilfred had been gone for hours, but in reality, he reappeared in less than twenty minutes.

Dix and Bubba pulled the other boat up close to them just in time to see Wilfred surface. The big man's eyes behind the mask were wide. He produced three objects wrapped in cellophane. They were off-white in color. Dix and Petersen gave each other a knowing nod.

Before anyone could comment, Wilfred said, "The whole bow and transom of the boat is full of these. It's definitely *Gray Ghost*."

The detectives looked at each other again and simultaneously said, "Oh shit."

CHAPTER FIVE

Wilfred's discovery forced Dix and Petersen to shift from fishing into police work mode.

Dix spoke first. "Our problems are many. The biggest is our lack of jurisdiction. The local police are definitely going to want this case. However, they're probably not prepared for anything this big. A substantial load of narcotics like this surely means cartels or Colombians are involved. If the United States has no solutions for dealing with them, it's likely the Bahamians don't either."

Bubba, Dix, and Petersen discussed the jurisdiction issue awhile, but couldn't come up with a way of justifying their involvement. They finally decided the largest problem now was what to do about the wreck and the contraband.

They'd discovered a crime scene, which also meant more headaches. Paperwork, confusion, and frustration lay ahead. Dix wanted to report the situation immediately to the Royal Bahamian Police Force, but Petersen wanted to search the area for more clues.

"Sharing the information with the locals would generate phone calls to the U.S. Navy, Royal Navy,

Royal Netherlands Navy, and Coast Guard. The red tape that kind of storm would generate would take months to sort out, providing any suspect or suspects ample time to escape," Dix argued.

"But the speedboat could reveal clues as to who killed Sean and Preston." Petersen watched, knowing Dix's analytical mind was probably bouncing theories and hunches around his brain.

Wilfred's eyes brightened. "We could fetch the speedboat from the ocean floor and store it without anyone knowing. You could conduct a private investigation. Let's mark the location with my GPS unit on the fish finder and return with the proper equipment after dark." He turned to Dix. "We'll use the moon for light. We should have the wreck up in less than an hour. Besides, we already have the boats, airbags, night vision goggles, and other necessary equipment in a safe place."

Why do these guys seem to have so many resources?

The four agreed, regardless of the outcome, further secrets were forbidden. Their goal formed an instant bond between them.

"What do you think?" Petersen asked Dix. He'd waited for this fishing trip for six years but felt compelled to help the locals now that they were involved.

"This could get ugly... quick. That load of cocaine and two murders makes this more than a simple drug deal gone wrong. We may have stumbled upon a sophisticated operation run by someone with vast knowledge of the narcotics world." It passed briefly in his thoughts that solving the case would be good for his career. *Maybe it would be enough to get promoted.*

Dix nodded. "This discovery would be one of the biggest seizures from Caribbean waters in a long time. But running an independent investigation in foreign waters?"

Petersen knew his partner didn't follow the rules all the time, but they were currently in the Bahamas, out of their jurisdiction. "We probably have no business getting involved in Bahamian drug trafficking problems," he conceded.

"I thought I was on vacation." Dix sighed. "I want to help, and the case is intriguing, so I guess I'm in." Dix pointed to the packages sitting on the deck and turned to Wilfred. "Wilfred, at the risk of sounding stupid, did you find those on the same speedboat you believe Sean and Preston were in when they were killed?"

Wilfred nodded. "Yes."

"Was there any evidence down there, such as registration markings, that may be helpful?" Wilfred nodded his head again.

"Well," Dix said, "It seems we all have a choice. We can leave one boat here to mark the spot while the other goes to get help. Or, we can put that off a bit, keep an eye out for spectators, and gather more information. Of course, then we have to decide how much of what we find, *if* we find anything at all, we should share with the local authorities. As far as I can tell, we wouldn't break too many laws by postponing the announcement of Wilfred's discovery. But make no mistake about it, we'll have to tell them eventually."

Petersen nodded. "I say we kindly ask Wilfred to dive once more to gather additional evidence."

Bubba, who up until this point had just watched and not said much, finally opened his mouth. "Will, ask them what dey need from *Gray Ghost* and go down to get it."

Dix assumed his natural role of lead investigator. "Listen, Wilfred, we need to figure out where the boat originally came from and where it was most likely headed. The closest spot I can think of is my neck of the woods, Miami. Florida requires Class II boats to have a registration decal on the port side and a painted registration number on both sides, usually all black and in three-inch block letters. If we're lucky, there will be an HIN on the outside of the transom."

Wilfred looked confused. "An HIN?"

"Sorry, that's short for Hull Identification Number." Dix chuckled. "I've always loved boats but never thought all my knowledge about them would be worth much. At the moment, I'm glad I know what to look for."

Dix and Wilfred spoke some more while Bubba and Petersen began to examine the packages Wilfred had brought up.

After grabbing a new tank, Wilfred entered the water again.

CHAPTER SIX

Coast Guard Lieutenant Commander Jim "Bloodhound" Calhoun stood on the bow of *Venturous,* a new Coast Guard Cutter. He was enjoying a very expensive cigar while he and the crew were finishing a fifty-day tour of the Caribbean. The cigar was a personal reward as he and the men had performed very well earlier in the day.

About a month had passed since the Coast Guard had intercepted a substantial load of narcotics headed for the United States. Contributing to the legend, the Coast Guard's Bloodhound laid claim to over sixty major drug interdictions, more than triple any other individual. Not only did he have a knack for sniffing out contraband, but he apprehended the smugglers with precision and ease.

Today's seizure was number sixty-one. Everyone on the cutter was talking about the ordeal since it was the Bloodhound who'd suggested moving south when recent intelligence suggested moving north to locate suspected illegal contraband. Bloodhound had told the Captain he had a hunch about a large amount of narcotics heading north toward Miami from Jamaica. He knew his old friend, the *Venturous's* captain, trusted his instinct. So the command to redirect to the south was given.

Seven hours later, a Stingray helicopter was deployed, as well as a few prototype boats. They'd intercepted a speedboat containing 500 kilos of cocaine and 100 pounds of heroin. Lieutenant Commander Jim Calhoun felt good about himself. The crew was raving over the accuracy of his sniper shot, which had disabled the fleeing speedboat. No Coast Guard casualties. That was the best news. *The brass loves it when no one dies*. As customary, Jim Calhoun had just provided the following detailed report to the Captain.

OPERATIONS REPORT:
On April 23, 2012, at approximately 1530 hours, a prototype boat, a Long Range Interceptor (LRI) in the final stages of testing, launched from the Cutter *Venturous* armed with .50 caliber machine guns and several Coast Guard seamen toward a previously fleeing vessel suspected of containing illegal contraband. The men had trained many hours and done hundreds of drills; however, this was a live-fire event. The suspected smugglers' vessel had been previously disabled by sniper rounds to the vessel's engines fired by Jim Calhoun. The Coast Guard units converged on the suspects quickly.

After the vessel was disabled, the two suspects on the speedboat were observed arming themselves. Each of them racked rounds into their AK-47s and donned flak jackets with full body armor. One of them retrieved a rifle fitted with a grenade launcher from the storage compartment of the speedboat. This area was later confirmed to be a modified weapons cache. The suspect chambered a 40 mm round into the launcher and appeared to say something to the other suspect.

Lt. Commander, Jim Calhoun and the spotters on the LRIs were not prepared for their aggressive actions. None of the Coast Guard personnel involved in this incident has been involved in a live-fire event except Calhoun, who confirmed with the advancing units that this was not a simulated drill. Based on the actions of the men in the vessel, it appeared a firefight was inevitable.

Rookie Coast Guard Seaman, Todd Ross, later reported he felt his heart race as he taped the firing mechanism for the .50 caliber machine gun mounted on the bow of the LRI with his fingers. Seaman Ross stated he had tunnel vision because all he could see was one of the AK-47s in the hands of one of the suspects. It should be noted that Seaman Ross performed his duties superbly and followed all directions and procedures from his superior officers.

Calhoun reminded everyone over the air not to engage the suspects on the disabled boat until they were fired upon first or the men trained their weapons on Coast Guard personnel. The recording of this announcement and all other radio transmissions has been retained per protocol.

The suspects on the disabled vessel were seen to look at each other and grin. Both suspects then swung their weapons toward Coast Guard personnel and began shooting at the advancing Coast Guard boats and also the helicopter Jim Calhoun was in. The first rounds from both suspects slapped the water near the incoming boats, but the boats continued. Seaman Ross said he saw rounds from the suspects pierce the water to the left of the LRI he was in. Observing the attack, Jim Calhoun radioed, "Green, go, go, go."

Seaman Ross fired a flurry of rounds at the suspects after being ordered to return fire. The .50 caliber rounds swept from left to right and finally caught the front of the boat. Ross stated he stopped firing when he believed the boat had been disabled.

One of the suspects raised the 40 mm grenade launcher and propelled a round at the helicopter. Jim Calhoun simultaneously squeezed the trigger of his sniper rifle, hitting the suspect in the chest. This suspect has been confirmed deceased.

The other suspect grabbed a .45 Glock from his hip and squeezed the trigger. The round traveled through his skull and out the other side. The final suspect has been confirmed as deceased by his own hand.

The incident ended at 1532 hours when Jim Calhoun announced over the radio, "All units stand down, repeat, stand down."

Both LRIs arrived at the disabled speedboat just after the last suspect committed suicide. The Stingray helicopter carrying Jim Calhoun returned to *Venturous* as it was low on fuel.

Coast Guard Seaman Ross and his partners needed most of the remainder of the day to process the contraband located on the vessel. Personnel recovered roughly 500 kilos of cocaine, a hundred pounds of heroin, illegal

rifles, ammunition, and a few bundles of cash estimated to be a million dollars. No identification was located regarding the two deceased suspects. All efforts will be made to identify the suspects once their remains are brought ashore.
END OF REPORT.

Beyond the obvious highlight of the seizure, the events made Calhoun, and by extension, the Coast Guard, look very good. It also helped justify the seventeen billion dollar Deepwater Project he'd helped push through Congress.

He smiled, knowing drug interdictions such as these made the politicians, and the voters, very happy. With the proposal for the project calling for ninety-one ships, thirty-five planes, and thirty-four helicopters and costly upgrades to the forty-nine cutters and ninety-three helicopters already in service, Calhoun realized he would need every bit of support he could muster to help the cause gain momentum. Positive media coverage was essential to promote the Coast Guard. However, he still felt a few more solid interdictions like the one today would be required to have any chance of getting enough votes for the project funding.

Calhoun was joined by several of his close friends on the bow of the ship as he finished briefing the Captain and handed him the report. The wind had picked up, making it difficult to light their cigars. Calhoun shielded his with his body and lit it. The others quickly followed his lead. These cigars had special meaning as they were recently seized from the captured speedboat listed in his report.

Soon after the first puffs, war stories began and expensive whiskey was poured. Calhoun focused on swirling the contents of his drink slowly around and around to help melt the single ice cube. He inhaled deeply on the cigar and found it to be smooth, with a clean burn. He wondered if Fidel stepping down would open trade up in Cuba, at least as far as cigar exportation was concerned. *The poor bastards who died today must have been rather well connected.*

Calhoun admired men with a taste for the exquisite. Unfortunately, the two dead men had chosen the wrong path. They wouldn't run dope again, that was for sure. *Regardless, none of my sentimental crap does them any good now.*

A discussion among the other men on the cutter about malfunctioning Unmanned Aerial Vehicles (UAVs) got his attention. The Captain and his crew often deferred to Calhoun because he was widely considered the expert when it came to technical systems, particularly computer and network communication with the fast unmanned aerial vehicles.

Calhoun had spent two years at MIT before finding himself bored and unchallenged, forcing him to move on to other things. From there, he'd landed in the Marines. Before long, he'd been selected for Special Ops missions, received the extensive training required for the various jobs he was assigned and spent a lot of time on foreign soil.

On this occasion, he explained to the rapt audience his theory about what was needed to prevent the UAVs from occasionally crashing into the ocean without any indication as to why.

Shortly into the discussion, his cell phone began vibrating in his chest pocket.

"Gentlemen." He retrieved his phone and glanced at it. "At the risk of boring you to sleep, I'll spare you of the required adjustments needed for the program to work efficiently. I have an important call to take. How about we meet for dinner?"

The men nodded and turned to walk toward the entrance to the ship's bridge while Calhoun answered his call.

CHAPTER SEVEN

Without the use of a high-powered microscope or a trained criminalist to inspect the cocaine, the three packages sitting on the Coleman cooler in Wilfred's boat looked just like thousands of other kilos the detectives had seen before. Each was wrapped several times in clear cellophane. It appeared they were stamped with a symbol, but without removing all the layers of plastic wrap, none of the men could begin to guess at what it might be. Then there was the question of whether or not knowing the information would help their investigation.

They decided to carefully open one package to get a better look. They discussed who would rewrap it to make it appear as though it hadn't been tampered with. Bubba said he'd take care of it. Since Bubba had volunteered to close it, they all agreed he should be the one to open it.

Bubba retrieved a pair of cloth sun gloves he used to protect his hands and slowly began the process of unwrapping one of the packages.

Dix wondered why *he* didn't think to bring gloves like Bubba's. He glanced at Petersen, who shrugged.

The contents were fairly mundane. It looked to be about the standard size of a kilo, two point two pound, pressed block of off-white, pure cocaine. Stamped squarely in the middle of the brick was a horse head emblem, about two inches tall and three inches wide. It was dark red in color.

Dix pointed to the image. "Have you ever seen that mark before?"

Petersen shook his head. "Nope."

Dix looked at Bubba. "You ever see anything like this?"

Bubba paused in his work. "Actually, I heard of the red horse head before."

"Where?" Dix was interested.

Petersen said, "I don't care how or why you've seen something like this before, Bubba, but can you tell us anything that might help?"

Bubba looked sheepishly from one detective to the other. "Our older brother used to run coke to Miami. He told me some of it was marked with red horse heads on it."

Dix shook his head. "Can we talk to him? See if he has some info that may be helpful?"

Bubba looked away. "No, you can't. He's dead."

"Man, I'm sorry to hear that." Dix shook his head.

Taking a deep breath, Bubba looked at Petersen and Dix. "I know people on the island who still run coke. I'll ask around when we get back to see when anyone last saw kilos with red horse heads on them."

The big man looked over the side of the boat where Wilfred still swam in the water below. Then he straightened. "I'll tell you what I know so far. There's a white guy known as the Caller. Don't know who he is. Supposed to have a lot of money from drug running. Maybe American. Pays locals to move his stuff from Jamaica and Bahamas to Miami. He's been in Andros for about twenty-five years. Never been caught. Nobody knows who he is. But he's lucky and gets most of his stuff through to the U.S."

The detectives glanced at each other, then back at Bubba.

Dix spoke first. "How does it work?"

"Someone gets a call. Guy's voice sounds weird and he doesn't say much. Number's always blocked. He's careful and good at what he does."

Petersen whistled. "Sounds pretty sophisticated.

"Near as I can tell, the head guy has to know something about how the feds work. Maybe he's a fed or local narc," Bubba added.

Petersen looked puzzled. "Why the connection with the feds or local narcs?"

Dix interrupted. "What about the Coast Guard, U.S. Navy, or Royal Navy?"

Bubba shrugged. "Could be them too. Whoever he is, he got trained on what not to do."

Dix figured Bubba was probably right, and it bothered him tremendously. The thought of someone wearing a badge or protecting the U.S. from narcotic smuggling involved in such an elaborate operation was something he feared would happen with all the sequesters, pay cuts, layoffs, and terrible morale in federal, state, and county law enforcement recently. But this guy had gotten into the narcotic business, probably for the money, well before all the problems in law enforcement began.

Petersen shrugged as Dix turned to him. "I'm having second thoughts about continuing this. The situation is already extremely sticky, and now two off-duty cops from Miami are knee deep in the middle of a major Bahamian problem."

Petersen raised his eyebrow. "Let's wait and see."

Dix nodded. He rubbed his temples as he felt a headache coming on.

They cracked open a few beers, shared the fresh tuna sandwiches from the cooler, and enjoyed the sunshine. Dix feared it might be the last time they'd be able to relax until this was all over.

Meanwhile, below them, they knew Wilfred was busy searching for clues.

Bubba pointed. "Here he comes now." He was obviously relieved to see his brother was okay.

When he surfaced, Wilfred immediately asked for something to write with.

Dix pulled a ballpoint pen from his fishing bag and Petersen produced a crumpled up napkin from his pants pocket.

Wilfred didn't wait to begin talking as Dix wrote. "BEX 571 something, something, B6 06. Port, red square decal, expires 02-08, Florida. Definitely a bunch more coke down there. The whole front of the boat and the side storage area is full of kilos."

Dix was impressed with what Wilfred had remembered. He wasn't too sure how far he could run with the new information, but he had a retired cop friend at the Florida DMV who was a whiz.

He carefully put the napkin and pen into his shirt pocket. "Good work, Wilfred. Why don't you get some food and drink? We already ate." Bubba and Petersen helped remove the diving gear. Wilfred looked beat and desperately in the need of some rest. Two solid dives had been completed with some results, but the physical burden was all over Wilfred's face.

However, Dix, in full detective mode, decided to question Wilfred further. "Hey Wilfred, did you see anything else down there?"

"Not that I can remember right now. You want me to dive again?"

Petersen stepped in. "We've got enough to go on. Let the guy rest. We've spent too much time poking around out here anyway. Although I'd love to chase a few more bonefish, we're gonna have to move quickly before this whole thing blows up."

Wilfred looked exhausted. "Besides, I can't think of anything else helpful right now. I really just want to eat my sandwich, drink some water, and rest."

Dix nodded. "You're right. Sorry, Wilfred. I get going and have trouble slowing down."

Wilfred quickly finished his meal, and then he and Bubba fired up the Yamahas and took their clients back to the lodge to freshen up. Dix watched as they got closer to land and was able to see more wildlife as the sun began to dip. *Shame to let narcotics take away from the real beauty of the island.*

CHAPTER EIGHT

A. M. Thomas, Special Ops, retired, had been a mercenary for hire for the better part of three years. His most recent contract, which he received through secure lines, was to locate, disable, and retrieve a speedboat named *Gray Ghost*. He was not told what was in the boat, but his experience in these things made him theorize it would be narcotics. His employer had said it contained *precious cargo*. Thomas studied the mission and classified it as moderately challenging. He would be paid handsomely when it was over.

However, due to a slight miscalculation and a somewhat errant .50 caliber round, he found himself in an undesirable situation. He'd successfully located the vessel and disabled it. But he'd failed to retrieve it. Therefore, until he got the speedboat, the lucrative contract would not be fulfilled.

He'd spent the last three days slipping into an area along the water under the cover of darkness to observe the general location where the boat had sunk. Each day, he slowly and meticulously got into position to monitor the water above where *Gray Ghost* lay at the bottom of the ocean. In his hotel room, he guessed at the coordinates of the speedboat based on his calculations while looking at an underwater topographical map of the area, and comparing it to where he was when he'd shot the two occupants of the boat.

Thomas looked at his handheld GPS unit. The temperature was rising, and he was getting warmer underneath his light-duty ghillie suit. That particular type of suit was commonly used by snipers to blend into their surroundings. Thomas had modified it to hold a medium-size hydration unit which he kept filled with cold, refreshing water. In his small chest pouch, he had nuts and a granola bar.

Near as he could figure, the closest house, and, therefore, most threatening, was about a half mile southeast of his location. It was occupied by a large family. Kids in the house were his biggest concern because they seemed curious and were always out and about.

He observed two teenagers take the smaller children away at about seven every morning. The teenagers returned about seven forty-five alone.

Before this little bit of activity, Thomas had been bored out of his mind. As he got older, he grew more impatient with waiting. He welcomed the small break, but it also meant he had to be more cautious.

Around eight-thirty that morning, he noticed Coast Guard boats arrive fairly far north of the general area of the sunken vessel. *If anyone stumbled upon the target, it would be these guys*. Thomas was curious as to why the Coast Guard was spending so much time in the area. He was not sure anyone had reported the boat he'd sunk as stolen or missing. On the third day, he figured out why. He watched as two bodies were lifted out of the water, assuming they were the men he'd killed. When the first body came completely out of the water, Thomas saw there was no head. *That must be the first guy I got*. That discovery alone would force the Coast Guard to investigate. They'd wonder where the bodies came from.

As a matter of protocol, and to keep news reporters off their back, Thomas thought the only real question was how long the Coast Guard would hunt for a boat that might or might not be there. He'd worked a few operations with Coast Guard teams in the past when he was a legitimate sniper. He'd learned how they operated.

As it turned out, the crew left the area in about six hours. As Thomas had anticipated, the Coast Guard's search efforts were unsuccessful. The deep water in the area would require weeks to search properly if there even was a boat involved. This was time the Coast Guard did not have. Also, one of the bodies they found had been decapitated and the other nearly so. Thomas hoped it would look to the Coast Guard like a cartel body dump.

Before he had time to breathe a little easier, Thomas noticed a small fishing boat enter the area he was watching. He presumed it was a local guide with a client. It headed directly toward the area he'd marked on his handheld GPS unit as the likely location of *Gray Ghost*. Several of these flats boats moved over the northern end of Andros, searching for tarpon, bonefish, and permit. It was a big time business for the locals and for some investors from the United States who provided the financial backing for several of the larger hotels. The sight of the boat didn't cause him much concern at first.

He watched as the boat slowed down over a flat. A slender, black man jumped up to the tower with a push-pole in his hand. Thomas pegged him as the guide. The client, a middle-aged white guy with a goatee and long hair, sprang to his feet and began manipulating a rod and reel. Through his high-tech binoculars, Thomas could see the guys were excited. Almost immediately, he noticed their bodies tense. He had been trained to read lips while working Special Ops, but the guide and angler were hardly moving their mouths.

Watching the angler work out some line and cast, he paid closer attention. The guy brought in a bit of line, paused and set the hook. Both men became extremely boisterous and began dancing around the front of the boat. But within a few seconds, it was all over. The man on the tower was laughing uncontrollably, and the fisherman was obviously pissed off. *Musta lost it.*

Thomas quietly chuckled, thinking the angler might have just blown his one and only shot at a fish during his eight thousand dollar trip. After a couple minutes, the guide was back on the tower, prowling for fish, and the angler was ready for another go.

The sniper wondered if those bozos had any idea they were close, too close now that he thought of it, to something worth more than they could ever dream about.

He watched the man pole the flat slowly. Thomas determined these guys were a very low threat, so he began surveying the rest of the area for potential problems. He was financially motivated to retrieve the boat and its contents. It had taken him three days to procure the resources and assistance to make it happen, and he was growing impatient while lying in the ghillie suit. Then again, the suit was the only thing keeping him hidden from the locals. He watched as children casually rode bikes along the partially paved road, laughing and having fun.

Sometimes they stopped at a little fruit stand to get a quick snack.

    About once an hour, a Royal Bahamian Police Force vehicle slowly rolled by the cluster of small houses to his left. The officer driving the car appeared to be as bored as he was. An ocean liner lazily cruised several miles offshore headed west. Ten minutes later, Thomas panned back over to the guys fishing the flat and felt like he'd been kicked in the stomach.

    A second boat had joined the first one there. It appeared the men were having a discussion and looking or pointing at the water.

    This isn't good. He noticed weights for a dive belt and an air tank canister on the bow of one of the boats. They hadn't been there before. Thomas suddenly realized one of the four men might dive.

    He blinked and raised the binoculars back to his eyes. He counted three men. The fourth must have gone underwater because he couldn't see him. *Shit.*

    Realization hit. The situation might have become a real problem. His head jerked and rose from his secure location. The action ruffled the ghillie suit. *Calm down, dammit.* He exhaled and took a deep breath which relaxed him, but only momentarily. Thomas was not sure if these guys were poaching for conch, or if they were actually diving near the speedboat. It was impossible to know where the two flats boats were in relation to where the man was diving. He did not have the coordinates of the two fishing boats so he couldn't compare their location to that of *Gray Ghost*.

Thomas trained the powerful scope of his sniper rifle on the chest of the puzzled looking fisherman with the goatee and long hair. The man leaned over the back of the boat. If Thomas needed to squeeze off a round to eliminate the guy, it would be okay. The rifle had a sound suppressor, which allowed it to be fired fairly quietly. However, Thomas would have liked to have his other sniper rifle. It was almost undetectable when shot. But, he'd destroyed and disposed of it after killing the two Bahamians.

The sniper watched as the goateed fisherman glanced from the water at his watch and back to the water. Quite a bit of time went by, and the guy repeated this action several times. The fact he continually stared at the water confirmed for Thomas that the last of the four men had dived in.

Finally, the diver surfaced. Thomas trained his scope on the man, but before he could get zeroed in, the hull of the flats boat moved between him and the diver, preventing a shot.

Thomas trained the crosshairs from his scope back and forth from man to man. He could easily have taken all of them out before they had time to react.

Even the diver wouldn't be safe forever in the water. Eventually, he'd have to come out, at which point, he'd be dead along with his friends. If the diver swam all the way back to shore while pushing the flats boat for concealment, he'd remain hidden, but it didn't seem physically possible. Thomas dismissed that scenario.

However, he was afraid to fire three rounds at the other men, even with the high-end sound suppressor. Not in daylight. Someone might discover his location. That wasn't a wise choice.

When he was younger and faced with life or death decisions, he'd never hesitated. It was why he had such a distinguished sniper career. Now he found himself trying to figure out his best option to retrieve the speedboat without giving up his location. Compromising his own safety was not an option. Thomas wanted to confer with his boss, but retrieving his cell phone might alert someone to his location.

Thomas had already killed two men on this mission. In that moment, he decided four more might be necessary. It would ensure no witnesses, which made things cleaner.

He watched as the diver handed the man with a goatee what looked like a small object wrapped in plastic. Might be something as trivial like a ham sandwich or more interesting... like a kilo of cocaine. Two more packages followed from the diver in the water up to the man standing in the boat. Not much doubt in Thomas's mind at this point. The diver had located *Gray Ghost*. *God damn it. How else could this get screwed up?* No more indecision. He decided they all needed to die, right then.

Thomas double-checked the distance and his rifle for any imperfections, also the wind measurements. He shot better from right to left, so he trained the scope squarely in the back of the man farthest to his left and drew in a breath to help steady the rifle. He planned to slowly squeeze the trigger, watch the others panic, line them up, and take them out. Exhaling, Thomas drew in another breath and moved his finger to the trigger. *These poor bastards*. As his brain told his right index finger to move, he heard what sounded like a twig cracking off to his right. He exhaled slowly and froze. *Probably just a rabbit or bird*. There was no way anyone who figured out his location could get to him before he knew it. *I'm re- tired Special Ops. Ain't no way these island bozos could get to me*. He let his guard down slightly and began breathing more normally. It had taken close to five minutes before Thomas was ready again to eliminate the four men in the two boats.

When he checked the image in the scope again, he saw the boat. He counted all four men this time. The diver had exited the water and was eating a sandwich. Thomas lined up on the man in the dive suit and began controlling his breathing again for another clean shot. *This needs to be accurate.*

He drew in a final breath and again heard an odd sound. This time it came from just two or three feet behind him. Holding his breath, he froze. It was too late. He heard and felt the air space around his head push across the ghillie suit as he was crushed along the temple with a blunt object.

* * * *

A teenage boy, his father, and uncle picked up Thomas's unconscious body and carried it to their home. In the back yard was a small two-room shed painted blue and green. They moved Thomas into the back area. He was shoved into a straight-backed metal chair in the windowless room, with a single bulb hanging over his head. They tied his hands together and bound his ankles to the chair legs with rope. Then one of them placed a handkerchief over his eyes as a blindfold and stuffed a towel in his mouth and duct taped it in place as a gag.

The captured man was breathing but unconscious. Significant bruising and swelling blossomed along the right side of his head.

His captors unloaded Thomas's rifle and placed it and the ghillie suit in a locked cabinet in the other room of the shed.

"He's more valuable alive than dead." The father explained to the other two who had worn puzzled looks on their faces.

They left the sniper inside the shed, secured the door with two deadbolts, and returned to the house.

The father walked to the front door and stepped outside. He raised the binoculars and noticed two of his friends, Bubba and Wilfred Jones, sitting in their boats talking to their clients. He thought it odd their clients weren't fishing. "What the hell is a sniper doing on the island? And why the hell was he watching Bubba, Wilfred, and their clients?" He heard his own voice and realized he'd spoken aloud.

He watched awhile longer, but didn't see anything unusual, except the group continued to talk, not fish.

Picking up his phone, he placed a call to Bubba, hoping the big man had his cell with him and service was available.

CHAPTER NINE

Petersen looked at Dix as they reached the dock. "We didn't do much actual physical labor, but man, I'm beat. How 'bout you?"

Dix replied, "Me too. I think I used my brain too much today, and it's only five o'clock. That means I'll be useless the rest of the evening."

"Isn't that the case most of the time?" Petersen chuckled. "You must really be tired. You don't often give me an opening like that."

They stepped off the boats.

Dix momentarily watched the rustling palm trees. He sniffed and could smell fresh conch in a fryer. "I could eat a bunch of those."

"Me too. And I could wash them down with a couple of icy beers," answered Petersen finally feeling less sick.

Dix raised his eyebrow. "After last night, you'd better stick to soda."

Petersen shrugged. "As long as it's got a little rum in it, I could probably manage."

"We've got time. If we work hard and catch a couple breaks, we might make a dent in the case. Should we call our sergeant and fill him in on what's happened?"

"Are you nuts? I think you're the one who needs a stiff drink."

Martin waited at the end of the dock and greeted them as they approached. "Guys, what's up? You're back awfully early."

Dix looked toward the main lodge. He noticed Suzie watching from the shadows. "Martin, the strangest thing happened. I hooked and landed the bonefish of a lifetime about the time Petersen was vomiting all over the ocean. Bubba decided to check on Wilfred and found him diving off a bonefish flat. After that, things got very interesting."

Martin raised an eyebrow. "Come on then, let's eat and drink and you can share your story."

Petersen held up his hand. "Sounds great, but I think I'll take a shower first and brush my teeth."

Dix nodded. "Martin, I'd like to shower before dinner, too. I'll let Bubba tell you about what's in the cooler."

Martin looked curious. "What? Does it have anything to do with Sean and Pres?"

Dix waved. "See you later." Then he and Petersen turned toward their cottage.

Forty-five minutes later, they were clean and getting dressed. Petersen put on a fish polo shirt and tan cargo shorts with flip-flops. Dix wore a Tommy Bahama floral print shirt, khaki shorts, and tennis shoes. They each grabbed a cold beer and headed to the main lodge.

Bubba and Wilfred met them in the lobby.

Dix looked them over. He noticed Wilfred had changed his shirt and Bubba changed into what looked like a track suit. "You guys look and smell a hell of a lot better than when we left you."

Bubba grinned. "We used a spare cottage to clean up. Always carry extra clothes in da car for after fishing. Martin usually feeds us." He patted his large stomach.

They walked into the private dining room where the Hamiltons waited.

Dix was impressed with the dinner selection of fresh lobster, blackened Mahi Mahi, fried conch, fresh bread, buttered pasta, and beer. The meal was delicious. *It's too bad we're going to ruin this fantastic dinner once we spill the beans to Martin.* Dix hoped Bubba or Wilfred had some cigars to enjoy during their long discussions.

Martin looked around the table. "So, what's going on?"

Bubba and Wilfred looked at each other and said together, "I'm not doing it."

Petersen looked at Dix and said, "We both know who the better public speaker is. Go ahead, Bill.

Tell him what we know so far. Start with the discovery of the speedboat."

Dix paused as one of the other fishing guests, apparently oblivious, had wandered into the private dining room. Suzie escorted the man back to his cottage.

Bill motioned to Bubba and Wilfred. "Martin, these guys are amazing. They have a lot of connections here."

Martin nodded. "The island isn't that big. We all know a lot of people."

"Yes, but what I'm trying to say is they know more about what happened to your friends than you might expect."

Martin appeared confused. "What are you getting at? What do Bubba and Wilfred know about Preston and Sean's murders?"

"Since Wilfred drew the short straw and got Steve," Dix explained, "He spent the better part of the morning watching his client vomit. After a while, we could tell Steve wasn't going to wet a line. So Wilfred decided to search for the speedboat."

Martin looked at Bubba and Wilfred, who both nodded.

Dix swallowed a bite of lobster dripping in butter. "Steve got a little better as they day wore on, and like any good guide, Wilfred put him on some tailing bonefish. Steve actually hooked a fish, but his tippet snapped as the fly line caught on his wrist watch."

Martin forced a smile. "That doesn't answer my question."

Dix continued, "Long story short, Wilfred stumbled upon a sunken vessel. He made a dive down to it and learned it was a speedboat loaded with cocaine."

Martin looked shocked. "Is that what Bubba has in the cooler?" Dix nodded.

"That's crazy." Martin shot a disapproving look at Bubba and Wilfred. "Totally my fault," Dix replied. "I wanted to look at it, maybe find a link to something or someone, and to keep it as evidence."

"You should have put it back," Martin insisted. "Why didn't you put the narcotics back?"

Dix shook his head. "Even if we'd decided to put it back, Wilfred didn't have enough air left."

Bubba leaned forward. "Martin, we took care of it. It's gone already."

Martin seemed to relax. "How do you know this involved Sean and Preston?"

Dix looked at Wilfred, who nodded. "I hate to tell you this, Martin, but they were in serious debt, mostly from gambling and drug use. They owed a dangerous man close to one hundred thousand dollars. From time to time, they did small runs. This man relieved some of their debt, but it was supposed to be the last time. If it makes you feel better, they never did it while working for you. They never used your boats or gas, and they took every precaution to ensure there was no possible link to the lodge. The guys considered you a very good friend and didn't want to make problems for you or your wife."

Bubba nodded, then looked at Martin. "Yeah, and according to the local news, their bodies were recovered close to where we found the boat today."

Wilfred nodded. "I saw damage to the boat's engines. They looked shot up. The locals say Preston and Sean were shot."

Martin drank a long swig of beer. Their host was obviously perturbed.

Wilfred leaned forward. "I had a call from Sean the night before they were killed. He told me a small job had turned into a monster, and he was looking for help. Sean asked if Bubba and I could pick up a truck and trailer the next morning and move it." Wilfred glanced at Bubba for confirmation.

Dix pointed to Bubba and Wilfred. "They've told me they're not drug smugglers. I believe them. "

Picking up his beer, Martin said, "So what's next?"

"I have some ideas, but I have to think this through," Dix answered.

Martin said, "Whatever you need…"

Dix ate more fried conch and took a swig of beer. Then he stood. "Gentlemen, I need to make a phone call. We also need to discuss how and when we let the local officials know about all this. Wilfred, did any more numbers pop up in your head from the speedboat?"

Wilfred appeared thoughtful. "For some reason, forty-five keeps coming up. Try putting a four and a five in the first numbers I gave you. You may want to swap them, too."

Dix added the numbers to the back of the napkin and retreated to the guest cottage.

CHAPTER TEN

Based on the late hour, Dix realized he couldn't call the Florida DMV. Thankfully, he had retired Miami-Dade Police Department Sergeant Andrew Snead's home phone number. Snead had access at all times to such records because he was well-liked. By the time he retired, many people owed him favors.

Dix had been trained by Snead when he was a rookie cop. Over the years, Snead had been promoted and eventually became one of the most respected guys on the force. Wherever he could, Snead brought Dix along, and always found a way to get him good press and plenty of face time with the Miami-Dade Police Department administration.

They'd been involved in some big busts in Miami. Two of them involved serious firefights. In the chaos of the last bust, Dix had allowed a suspect to get behind him. The perpetrator raised his assault rifle to Dix's back. As he did, Snead squeezed the trigger of his AR-15, and all three rounds tore through the suspect. Dix turned just in time to see everything unfold and dive for cover. From that point on, Dix and Snead had become close.

Dix dialed Snead's number. It rang twice, and Snead's southern drawl came across the line. "How they hell are you, Bill?"

Dix told Snead about the amazing lodge they were at and said the fishing was as excellent as the website had reported. He even told Snead that he would have to come along the next time. Snead asked, "Well, I can't imagine you broke into your vacation just to brag about it. So what in Sam Hill do you really want?"

"Andy, can't a guy just call a friend to see how he's doing?"

"Tarnation. Any other local guy would, but I know that's not why you called. So spill it."

"You're right, as usual. I need a favor."

"Okay, but only if you promise to take me to the lodge you're braggin' about sometime."

"Deal." Dix quickly recapped for Snead, telling him about the murders aboard *Gray Ghost*, and the cargo lodged in it on the ocean floor.

"How's your buddy Steve?"

Dix was annoyed but guessed Snead needed time to process the information. "He's as obstinate as ever. Now, can I continue?"

"I guess. Remember, you're on your own dime. By the way, did you clue in the department on this?"

Dix paused. *He knows I didn't. He's joking, right?* "Uh, not yet."

"Good."

Dix sighed, and then filled in the remaining details. "So," Snead said, "Why are you calling me about this?"

"The boat had Florida tags," Dix replied.

"How is it you always end up under the dangdest dark cloud? You know I'll help, but are you sure this is what you want to do? Before long, several agencies could be all over this. Not to mention exploring the boat and removing the coke. Hell, you've already broken about a dozen laws."

"It feels like the right thing to do, Andy."

Snead chuckled. "Let me get some paper and a pen. You need the info for the registration ASAP?"

"The quicker, the better."

"Message received. Go with the numbers."

"This is what we have: BEX 571 space space, B6 06. Wilfred said the two spaces may be a four and a five. He also saw a red square decal on the port side of the boat that read, 'Expires 02-08, Florida.'"

"I can tell you the boat was last registered in Florida in 2006. I'll give you the rest when I run it out. I've got a friend working who might be able to check tonight. I'll get a hold of him and call you back. Okay?"

Dix was happy with the answer. "Absolutely, I'll keep the cell phone close by. Thanks a bunch, Andy."

"What are friends for?" The line went dead.

Surprised to find himself still hungry and thirsty, Dix decided to rejoin his friends in the main lodge. Evening was settling in as he walked along, too absorbed in the *Gray Ghost* and its cargo to notice the bright moonlight.

Back in the dining room, Dix slid into his seat. "Well, gentlemen, did I miss anything?" He helped himself to another cold beer and another lobster tail.

* * * *

Bubba stepped onto the deck from the kitchen and flipped his cell phone open. It made a chirping sound. His message tone. Bubba looked down at the screen. He didn't have one message. There were seven, and he'd missed ten calls.

He punched in the numbers and pressed the button to listen. All of messages were from his friend, Roger Fellows, a family friend who lived close to Bubba's parents on the north end of the island. Each message said Roger needed to speak to him urgently. If it had been one message, Bubba would have called Roger back later, but because there were seven, he figured it must be very important.

He'd started to dial the number when he saw Roger's beat-up blue station wagon scream up the dirt road to the lodge.

Hoping nothing was wrong with his parents, he grimaced at the vehicle. His mother had recently been diagnosed with cancer and had returned from the hospital after receiving chemotherapy treatments. She'd looked quite ill when Bubba last saw her. The doctors said they didn't know how long she had to live.

As the car got closer, it began to skid. Before it came to a complete stop, Roger was already out. He ran directly toward the main house. The dinner guests had heard the screech of brakes and came out to see what had happened.

Martin chuckled. "Nothing to be concerned about, folks. Just an old friend with poor driving habits."

Everyone except Dix and Petersen went back inside. Bubba approached Roger. "Man, what is it? You drivin' like a maniac."

Roger panted. "Well, mon, answer your damn cell phone and I wouldn't need to drive like that." Roger cautiously eyed Dix and Petersen.

Bubba said, "Come on. Out with it, mon." Bubba saw Roger examining Dix and Petersen. "It's okay, they're cool."

Roger hesitated a moment. "Okay, we need to talk somewhere private."

"How about the boat shack at the end of the dock?" Bubba pointed to the far south end of the property.

They grabbed a few beers and cigars and strolled to meet the others, trying to look casual.

Dix turned to Petersen. "This is a fine mess you got me into."

They argued all the way as to who was to blame for their involvement.

Roger opened a beer and sat down. "Bubba, this has nothing to do with your momma or papa." He motioned to the other chairs. "Get comfortable. This will take a while."

Roger looked at Dix and Petersen.

Dix held out his hand. "I'm Bill Dix, and this is my partner, Steve Petersen."

"I'm Roger Fellows. You should know I don't trust strangers, but since Bubba says you're cool, I guess you're okay."

Dix nodded. "Thanks."

Roger took another gulp from his can. "A few hours ago, my son, Tommy, was looking out at the sea as he was procrastinating about doing his homework. He thought he saw a piece of dry grass, about the size of a rabbit, move up and down. Tommy thought the grass seemed sort of strange. He said it looked like it didn't belong. He watched it for ten more minutes, but it didn't move again."

Roger stood up and started to pace. "Tommy was still curious, so he just kept staring out at sea and at the patch of grass. After a while, he got off his lazy butt and walked out toward where he thought he'd seen movement earlier. He got about a hundred yards away and saw it move again."

Bubba looked from Dix to Petersen. "His kid knows this whole island. If he said it didn't belong, then it didn't."

Roger nodded. "When it moved again, Tommy came to get me."

Bubba grew impatient. "Where you going with this?" He knew his friend was long winded.

Roger replied, "Damn, mon, you always want everything right now. I'm getting to it, and I'm sure it has to do with Sean and Preston."

Everyone froze.

Dix raised an eyebrow. "What makes you think that?" Roger didn't answer but continued. "So, like I said, Tommy thought something was up, so he backed off and came to get me. I went to see what he was looking at and watched for about ten, fifteen minutes. I didn't see a thing and was getting ready to tell Tommy he was crazy when I thought I saw movement through my binoculars. Sure as heck, it looked like a patch of longer grass and brush that was different than the surrounding area. At first I dismissed it, figuring I may be seeing things. But, since I'm into plants and such, and I wasn't doing much, I figured I'd go check it out anyway."

Roger took a deep breath and continued. "It took me a long time to get to about fifty yards from the patch. I was hoping to catch a rabbit, so I was real slow and deliberate. The patch began to take shape the closer I got to it. When I was about forty yards away, it was obvious the area didn't fit in." Petersen scratched his chin. "Why was that?"

"It was about the size of a person. I thought maybe someone tried to dump a body."

Dix leaned forward. "Do people dump bodies out here a lot?"

"No, but it happens sometimes." Roger shrugged. Peterson said, "Okay. So what else happened?"

Roger appeared to think a moment. "I grabbed my binoculars and looked out in the water in front of the shape." He pointed to the detectives. "I saw you guys in two boats. Except you weren't fishing, and I didn't see Wilfred."

The men looked at each other.

"Then I had a thought. Word on the street was Sean and Preston were killed by a large caliber round. Some folks speculated about a high-powered rifle. I stopped moving, thinking a person with a gun might be hiding there."

Bubba sat forward. "So then what happened?"

"I'm gettin' there. I didn't have my gun, but I spotted a two-by-four tucked in the dogwood bushes. I grabbed it as quietly as I could and moved closer. When I was about five yards away, I noticed the left side of the object raise and lower like it was breathing. This pretty much confirmed a live body was underneath. When I saw the barrel of a rifle come out, pointed in your direction, I didn't even think, I just swung down on the grass where I thought a head might be."

Bubba and Wilfred were shocked. Dix and Petersen just looked at each other and back at Roger.

"The guy must have figured out I was there just as my swing came down on him. He turned over enough for me to catch him right across the temple with my piece of wood, and out he went."

Bubba was concerned. "Did you kill him?"

Dix had his own questions. "Where's the body? What was he wearing? What did he look like?"

Petersen cleared his throat. "Calm down. Maybe the guy's alive." Everyone looked at Roger waiting to hear his reply.

Roger nodded. "He is."

Dix shook his head. "Roger, you saved our lives. That son of a bitch could have taken us out. Thank you."

Dix offered Roger his hand and then stood up. "I want to question the guy, at length, and then punch him squarely in the face. The asshole may have killed or was involved with killing Preston and Sean."

Roger motioned toward his car. "Let's take a ride. He's regained consciousness. Tommy and my brother are guarding him in my backyard shed. Oh, and one more thing, I haven't told the police about this yet."

Dix looked at Peterson and shrugged.

The detectives piled into Roger's vehicle, anxious to talk to the captive.

Bubba waved. "You can handle this." He headed back to the dining room as the car sped away.

CHAPTER ELEVEN

Jim "Bloodhound" Calhoun contemplated the contents of the brief, yet informative phone call he'd just completed.

He wasn't completely surprised, but he was disappointed.

According to his source, two significant problems had developed. First, the initiative for the Deepwater Project was shot down in the House of Representatives. Apparently, the money wasn't right, and the cost of the scheduled maintenance of the new equipment was unsettling to the people who had to sign the checks. Second, and more importantly, hiring the retired Special Ops mercenary turned out to be an egregious mistake.

One of Calhoun's biggest competitors from Columbia arranged to send a massive shipment of cocaine to Miami through the Bahamas. To maintain his control of narcotic distribution on the East Coast, Calhoun had planned to have the load hijacked. If all had gone well, the boat and its contents, worth close to one hundred million dollars, would be sitting in a slip registered to a fake owner in the port of Miami. But, it hadn't gone well.

A loss of this size would temporarily crush his opponent, and make others think twice about trying to move into his territory. The only contingency he hadn't prepared for was the mercenary failing, and worse, sinking the cargo.

The Deepwater Project could wait. In the meantime, the Coast Guard would get the funding necessary to remain the primary force patrolling the Caribbean, mostly because no one else was prepared or trained to do it as well.

Thomas had come highly recommended and had no idea who'd hired him, but he might be able to provide law enforcement with a clue to Calhoun's identity.

Calhoun took a deep breath and reminded himself to remain calm and focused when he called the sniper-for-hire. He would not pay the contract, and the guy could expect heavy penalties.

However, every time he tried to call Thomas, he got no answer.

This was unusual because Calhoun had used Thomas three times prior to this mission, and he always answered and returned calls quickly.

Calhoun grew more upset. Not knowing the current status of the situation was eating him up.

He felt his blood pressure rise. He had himself mostly to blame for relying on the aged sharpshooter. Now his entire operation was in jeopardy. Calhoun wasn't ready to let go of thirty years of diligent work and deception, just because of a little hiccup. Not yet anyway... *I'm going to have to take care of this myself.*

CHAPTER TWELVE

Dix's cell phone rang, waking Petersen in the rear passenger seat. He grabbed it from his pocket and looked at the screen. The call was from Snead.

He answered. "Speak to me, bud. What do you have?"

"You're in a good mood. Tell me what *you* got, and I'll tell you what I got."

"Deal. One of the locals apprehended a sniper."

"A what? Did you say sniper?"

"Yes, sniper. Before you ask what it means to this case, I have no idea. The locals assume the bastard murdered Sean and Preston."

Snead laughed. "Man, you step into shit no matter where you go."

Dix chuckled. "I have you to thank for that."

Snead grunted. "I've got your intel, but I don't know how helpful it'll be."

"I've got a short ride, so make it quick."

"The vessel is registered out of Florida. Miami to be exact. Registered owner is a female named Jackie Spears, with an address on Palm Drive. And before you ask, I already ran her. Near as I can tell, she doesn't exist. Looks like a phantom registration. I called my techie buddies to see if they could come up with anything else."

Dix was already ahead of his friend, wondering what the information meant.

"Hold on a second," said Snead. "What's up? I just got an instant message from one of my guys. He says he had to disable several firewalls and a worm virus which attacked his computer when he started his search for a Jackie Spears at that address."

"Jesus, this thing gets crazier by the minute."

"It's a hell of a sophisticated operation," replied Snead. "We haven't seen this level of complexity at the office.

Do you remember anything like it before you retired?" Dix wondered who could pull something like this off.

"We had the one case out of Miami, remember, where a guy led us on a wild goose chase. He had everything safeguarded on his laptop. He was a small time dealer, but he used lots of smokescreens and stuff."

"That's right. Didn't we have to send the laptop off to the FBI, and they sent it to the nerds at MIT to get into it?"

"Yep. Even those guys needed two damn days."

Dix had hoped to get a lead from the data he gave Snead, but it hadn't worked out. "Okay, so I won't know much for a few days, if at all."

"Don't get your panties in a wad. I still have a few tricks up my sleeve." Snead chuckled.

"Okay, I have to go. We're pulling up to where the locals stashed the guy they caught."

"Be careful." Dix strongly considered Snead's warning as he ended the call.

CHAPTER THIRTEEN

A young Bahamian man Dix assumed was Roger's son opened the front door of the house before the car came to a complete stop. He was dressed in black and armed with an MP-5 over his shoulder and a Colt .45 on his hip.

The house door closed, and Roger glanced over his shoulder. "We have company. Police on the left."

Dix nodded.

"They haven't driven down here for months."

Roger looked at the detectives. "No offense, guys, but let me do the talking if they stop."

A white van slowed to a crawl as it neared the house. The driver positioned the vehicle to block Rogers's car as it stopped. Two uniformed local officers emerged.

Roger flashed them a friendly smile. "Good evening, gentlemen. How are you?"

The older of the two, a light-skinned man with a thick British accent answered, "Hello."

His partner, much darker skinned and younger, nodded. Roger pointed to his visitors. "This is Mr. Dix and Mr. Petersen. They're guests at Turtle Cay Lodge. Bubba and Wilfred Jones took them fishing today and convinced them to try my famous guava jam rolls. Would you like a taste?"

The younger officer stepped forward. "Well, speaking about those rolls, that's why we're here. The commissioner is entertaining guests from the States and wondered if he could get some to impress his visitors."

Roger's grin broadened. "Is that all? I thought you were here to take me away."

Both officers chuckled.

Roger turned toward the house. "Wait here and I'll get a dozen for the commissioner."

The older officer walked back to the van and got into the driver's seat while the younger one asked if he could go inside to see how the rolls were made.

Dix heard the tension in Roger's voice when he said, "Sure." Dix decided to create a diversion. "If you don't mind my asking, what do you guys do for excitement on the island? After all, it's pretty small."

"What? You think the police don't have much to do here?"

Dix smiled. "I don't see how you could." The rookie Royal Bahamian police officer turned to Dix and Petersen while Roger slipped into the house.

The officer chuckled. "We have locals trying to get rich off tourists like you by picking their pockets. We deal with robberies and narcotics smugglers. There's a lot happening on this island, so we need to keep things quiet. Tourists would not come here as much if they knew about our issues."

Roger returned just as the officer concluded, "… and that's why we work so hard." The rookie grabbed the plate as the police radio came to life. "Got a call. Thank you."

He jumped in. The driver started up and the van sped back down the dirt road with lights and sirens blaring.

Petersen watched as they drove out of sight. Well, that was fun."

Dix grimaced at him, then turned to the others. "Don't mind him. He's an idiot."

Roger sighed. "The bastard in my shed slips in and out of consciousness. I don't know if he'll talk, but we should try." They entered the house.

Dix turned to Petersen. "Stay here while we go to the shed. Holler if there are any problems."

They circled the shed. At the door, Dix saw two armed men wearing black clothing. The entrance faced the back fence, so the men were not visible from the street. He recognized one as the guy they'd seen at the front door of Roger's home. Roger told the guards it was okay to let Dix in.

They hesitated.

Dix stepped in front of Roger. "Listen, boys, I'm here to help. I want to find out if your prisoner is the guy who killed Sean and Preston. If I really wanted to stir up some shit, I'd point out that you both forgot to take the safeties off your MP-5s. I'd have plenty of time to disarm you before you figured it out."

Roger chuckled, then pointed to the guy on the left. "This is my son and that is my baby brother. Guys, he's right. Get the safeties off just in case."

The guard Roger had identified as his brother spoke. "I think the man is awake, but he's pissed."

Roger grimaced. "He has big problems to worry about."

The guards stepped away. Roger removed a key from a chain around his neck and unlocked the door. He walked in, followed by Dix. They entered the second room and the sniper looked up but said nothing since he was still gagged.

Roger ripped the duct tape off to release the towel. The prisoner took a deep breath as Roger glared at him. "Just checking to see if you're alive."

The man in the chair looked from Roger to Dix. "Yes, barely. Do I get bread and water? I won't be much use to you dehydrated and famished."

Dix listened carefully. The guy's English sounded Midwestern. "Listen, prick, let's skip the formalities and get to the point."

"A fellow American. What a relief. Maybe you can convince them to give me something to eat. And maybe remove the blindfold as well."

"You'll get food and water when I decide they can give it to you. As for the blindfold..." Dix answered, motioning for Roger to take it off.

The guy blinked a couple of times. "Thanks. Now how about something to drink? I can talk better if I'm not parched. Besides, isn't providing sustenance to captives required?"

Dix shook his head. "That only applies during wartime. Since it appears you're a mercenary, whoever hired you won't be contacting local law enforcement to report you missing."

The prisoner sighed. "Well, if you're going to kill me, just do it. I've been in worse situations. This contract was supposed to be my last. I was going to retire."

Dix raised an eyebrow and stared at the man. "You retired once before I bet. Why are you doing contracts at your age?"

"Two daughters in college." He eyed Dix and smirked, "And I can still get the job done."

"That may be, but now you have major problems."

The shooter looked at the room, his hands, and his legs. "Maybe."

Dix watched as the sniper slowly slumped over, and he motioned for Roger to get the man a drink.

Roger left and returned with a glass of water and a large piece of bread which he fed to the prisoner.

When he was finished, he turned to Roger. "Was it you who got me good? What did you use, a piece of wood?"

Roger smiled. "Yes and yes."

"Snuck up on me. Didn't think it was possible. I watched you and your family and dismissed you as a threat. Apparently my judgment failed me."

Dix wanted to get on with the interrogation. They'd already wasted valuable time. "Let me tell you what I know. Stop me when I'm wrong."

"What? You're not going to ask my name, and who I work for, and what I was doing?"

Dix grabbed another chair from the corner and sat opposite the suspect. "I know most of that already. You were hired, most likely by the Caller, to hijack a large shipment of coke. It probably belonged to one of the Caller's competitors. You took the job and came to Andros Island intending to disable the boat and secure the cocaine. Unfortunately, you allowed the speedboat to get underway before you could intercede. So you figured you'd kill the occupants to stop it. I'm not sure if that was part of the contract or not."

Thomas tried lying first. "I don't know what you're talking about. I came here last night. I did take a contract from the Caller, but it was to fix someone else's mistake. All I was told was there was a vessel underwater containing precious cargo. I was provided GPS coordinates for the vessel and was scouting out the location to see how to retrieve the boat when I was smacked across the face."

Dix thought for a moment. "As you fired on the occupants, you accidentally disabled the vessel, and it sank. You jacked up the mission. To make up for your mistake, you offered to fix the situation quickly and quietly, which the Caller agreed to. You monitored the location and saw a flats boat arrive. After a while, one of the occupants left the boat and dove down to your sunken speedboat. As he came up, another boat arrived. So you were going to eliminate the people on the boats. For some reason, you moved around too much underneath your ghillie suit. That's what gave you away."

The prisoner remained in eye contact with Dix. "You keep saying I killed two people. It's not true. I admit I was going to kill the guys poaching in the area I thought the speed boat was in." He shrugged. "Business is business."

Thomas motioned with his head to Roger. "I paused, which enabled him to capture me."

Dix asked, "Where did you deploy from?"

"I was in Nassau diving. The details were sent to my iPhone. Arrived here about an hour later by boat."

Dix spoke quickly. "Where were you diving?"

The guy hesitated, then replied, "The Tongue of the Ocean."

Roger cleared his throat. "Dix. He's full of shit. The Tongue is about a mile off of the island we're standing on."

Dix stared at the suspect. "Thanks, Roger. As far as I'm concerned, unless he wants to tell us who the Caller is, you and your friends can do with him what you want." Then he softened his voice and added, "Listen, man, tell us what you know, and I'll do what I can to keep you alive. You know you have no other options. Prison or death."

The sniper closed his eyes. "Get me some aspirin, and maybe something more than stale bread, and I'll tell you what I know. No joke, I've had it. I choose prison, although I am not too sure I'll make it out of this shed alive regardless." Dix asked Roger to get the aspirin and some fresh food.

While Dix was alone, he leaned back in his chair. "Okay, who are you and what's your background?'

The sniper watched him closely. "M. A. Thomas. Retired Special Ops."

Dix nodded. "Just as I thought."

Roger came back with a can of soda, aspirin, and fresh fruit, which he gave to Dix.

"Untie his hands, but keep his feet tied to the chair legs. The door is locked, and there are no weapons here. Even if he escaped his bonds, he'd be dead as he stepped out of the shed."

Thomas popped the aspirins and drank the soda in one long gulp.

He peeled a banana slowly and began to eat it.

"Time is of the essence, Thomas. Finish that bite, and we'll continue."

Thomas chewed and swallowed. "Shoot."

Dix leaned forward. "Now, tell us what really happened."

"You got most of it right. I took out the men on the speedboat because I panicked after miscalculating my shot."

Roger punched Thomas twice in the stomach. Thomas doubled over in pain and groaned.

Roger said, "That's one for each of my friends, Sean and Preston. If I'd known for sure you were involved before I called Bubba, I'd have cut your fingers off and shot you with your own rifle. I'd kill you now, but I gave my word not to. I hope you rot in prison."

Roger wheeled around, fists clenched at his side, and left the room.

Dix didn't feel sorry for Thomas, but he had to get more information.

Thomas quickly reached over to grab Dix's leg, but Dix was quicker. He slammed his right elbow into the middle of Thomas's back. The blow knocked Thomas onto the ground with the chair still secured to his ankles.

Dix stood over Thomas glaring at him. "What the hell was that about? I'm not the enemy. You're lucky to be alive. The quicker you tell us what we need, the quicker we turn you over to the police."

Thomas gasped, "Help me up."

"Not until you tell me everything. Do you understand?"

Thomas groaned and nodded. "The Caller is American and most likely has military training. He has knowledge of drug trafficking trends and interdiction. He does his business through middlemen and uses only secured lines on a cell phone when he calls. He pays very well. Dix frowned. "You've done a lot of checking on this guy, haven't you?"

"I tried to figure out who he was because I wanted to have some dirt on him as protection."

"When was the last time you worked for him?"

Thomas groaned again, but when Dix made no move to help him, he took a breath and continued. "Over a year ago. I hadn't shot the rifle since."

"What else can you tell me about the Caller?"

"I think he works alone because I ran into roadblocks everywhere when I tried to track him down. I don't know much about computers, but when I tried to search for cell phone numbers I had and possible associates, my computer froze up and I had to take it to a local computer store to get it working again."

"Is there anything else you think could be helpful?" Dix was tired and wanted to get Thomas to the local cops.

"Whether I'm arrested or one of these men kill me, I think the Caller will send someone else to finish this mission. A hundred million is sitting on the ocean floor. The one person he told about it failed to return it to him. I don't know anyone who would pass up that much money. Someone else will come."

"You killed two men. I hope you rot in hell." Dix spat on the floor next to the sniper. Then he righted the chair and retied Thomas's wrists before he knocked on the door.

Roger unlocked it. "What now?"

"We turn this guy in. It's time to turn everything over to the local officers."

"All right. We'll take him out of the shed and transport him to the police department."

"Okay, let's go."

Roger's guards untied Thomas's legs from the chair and allowed him to stand to get his balance. After a minute, they started escorting him from the shed out to the backyard.

Thomas brushed past the two young men when he went through the door. His right hand was free of the rope Dix had loosely placed on him. With speed and agility, Thomas grabbed the gun from one of the armed guards and ran toward the side yard of the house. He had fired a few rounds in the direction of the house and the shed before he took cover behind an abandoned car surrounded by tall grass.

Everybody scrambled for cover as a round echoed in the air. A .223 caliber round caught Thomas on the left side of his body. The bullet tore through major organs and he slumped over dead next to the car.

Dix rushed from behind the shed to find Roger standing over Thomas's body.

Petersen ran from the house and approached the body, checking for a pulse, then turned to Dix.

"He's dead." Removing the rope from Thomas's left hand, he handed it to one of the young men looking over his shoulder. "Make this disappear."

Roger turned to his son. "Get the guy's gear from the shed." The only thing they kept was the handheld GPS with the coordinates to the speedboat.

The boy returned quickly. They put the ghillie suit back on Thomas's lifeless body. One of Roger's sons placed a Colt .45 close to the dead sniper's hand.

Petersen turned to the group. "Okay, who shot him?"

The son whose gun Thomas had stolen looked down. "I did."

Petersen nodded. "We need to come up with a story and then make sure everyone else goes along with it."

Fortunately, no one else had been injured.

Petersen spoke first. "We need to have a reason for shooting this guy. Here's what I'm thinking. Roger, we say you caught the guy and planned on calling the local police to turn him in. Before you could do that, the sniper grabbed your kid's gun and ordered him at gunpoint to let him go. The sniper became desperate and made a run for one of the cars parked out front. He turned and fired at the house, and Roger shot him to protect his family." The group nodded.

When everyone had agreed on their part in the story, Roger placed a frantic phone call to the police, telling the dispatcher he'd just shot someone.

Dix hoped their story would work. *With the secluded location and no other witnesses, we just might pull it off.* It was a crime scene, after all. He didn't feel good about Petersen compromising it, but he didn't see that he'd had a choice.

He could barely hear the steel drums from the celebration in town but realized their sound had probably covered the gunshots. Now police sirens grew louder than the drums.

Dix felt his cell phone vibrate and answered. "Stand by." He heard Snead's twang on the other end. "Hey bud, what's up?"

Dix took a deep breath, "Remember when I mentioned the sniper?"

"Yeah."

"Well, he gave us all kinds of information about this Caller guy. He confessed to killing Sean and Preston but claimed it was an accident. Then he got a hand free, took a gun, and escaped. He fired a few rounds at the house and was killed by a single round."

"What the hell you guys doing over there? Sounds like rookies at amateur night."

"Somehow, he got one hand free of the restraints I'd tied on him."

"How in tarnation did that happen?"

"The rope must have been a little loose."

"Didn't I teach you better than that?"

Dix knew it wasn't wise to argue with Snead.

"Well, he'd have spent the rest of his worthless life in prison or gotten the death penalty."

"Retirement has made you sour." Dix smiled.

"Hell, I was always sour. I let up on you because I liked you,"

"Okay, what do you have for me?"

"The computer guys are still messing with the leads I gave them. I did some research on the internet for variations of the name Jackie and Spears. Most hits were for ladies in the U.S. and the U.K. I read them all. One of the bios I read was rather interesting. A Jackie Lynn Spears was found in a car at the bottom of a lake, near Tallahassee, Florida, about six years ago. Her maiden name was Jackie Lynn Calhoun. Her late husband, who was considered the prime suspect in her murder, was named Arthur Spears, hence the name change."

Dix said, "Besides being murdered and found at the bottom of the lake, what makes her so interesting?"

"Don't interrupt, boy. They never figured out how Jackie Spears died, but murder was possible. The prime suspect was her husband. The detectives working the case couldn't sell the scraps of evidence they had to the District Attorney's office, and apparently, the husband was terminally ill with cancer at the time. Afterward, he miraculously recovered and moved on. He also remarried within a month."

"What's the status of the case?" Dix asked.

"Cold file. Just sitting in a basement somewhere."

Dix couldn't see the pieces fitting together. "So is there a connection?"

"Son, you need to learn a little patience. Here's the interesting stuff. Jackie Lynn Calhoun was the daughter of Coast Guard Lieutenant Commander Jim Calhoun. She was his only child. Her mother died when the girl was young, and Calhoun raised her alone."

"Are you talking about Bloodhound Calhoun?"

"I sure am. A few months after the husband was magically cured, he died under suspicious circumstances. Get this, his body was discovered in a car in the same lake as Jackie Spears. That case was also ruled a murder with no leads, no clues, no evidence, and no suspect. Seems like a professional job. The detectives didn't seem to look too hard either."

Dix said, "Did anyone ever question Bloodhound?"

"You're joshin' me, right? The guy's a living legend. He has the reputation of being a straight arrow. People were so busy consoling him for the loss of his only child, it probably never crossed anyone's mind to question him."

Dix thought about it for a second. "I guess you're right. Probably wouldn't have questioned him too much either."

He knew about Calhoun's reputation, not only in the Coast Guard, but among high-ranking politicians and law enforcement. No one had more information and understanding of narcotics trafficking in the United States, and probably on the planet.

He'd even written two books on the subject. The last Dix had heard, the guy was still actively patrolling the Caribbean as a Coast Guard Commander and pushing the Deepwater Project. Dix idolized Calhoun and had read his books to give him an edge when he interviewed for the narcotics task force.

Snead interrupted his thoughts. "I thought the whole thing stank to high heaven, so I dug a little deeper. Turns out, any and all records for Jim Calhoun's daughter were wiped clear off the face of the earth the day after her body was found. The techies say they aren't sure how this was done, but they're having fun trying to figure it out."

Dix whistled. "Man, how weird. Calhoun is so by-the-book, it's hard to even consider he might have had something to do with his ex son-in-law's death."

"I agree. There's absolutely no way he could have been involved. I don't think a man like that gets where he is to just throw it all away with something stupid like that."

"I've heard fathers sometimes go berserk when their children die, especially when they are murdered." Dix thought what he might be capable of doing if someone ever hurt his two children.

"Can you blame them?"

"I guess not. But, I don't think I'd go that far." Dix thought about his son and daughter. He decided he probably would kill someone if they harmed his kids.

"You can't say what you'd do in those circumstances. Anyway, I think it's time you guys let the locals in on this whole situation. It's getting worse by the minute, and people keep dying. I thought you guys were on vacation."

"You're right. In fact, the cops are on the way. I can hear the sirens."

Snead was sassy as ever. "You know I'm right."

Dix thought their conversation was over.

But Snead added, "Now that the sniper is dead, what are you going to do about his confession?"

"Why does it matter?"

"I think the victims' families might like closure."

Dix replied, "We took care of that. The local guy said he'd make sure they knew the truth."

"Sounds like you've got things under some sort of control for now. If I hear back from the computer junkies, I'll let you know."

"I appreciate all your help so far." The line went dead, and Dix hung up.

Dix decided it was time to notify the police about the coordinates of *Gray Ghost*. It would be easier to examine out of the water, and the Caller might come looking for his lost load. *If he does, we can nail the bastard. I bet he won't let one hundred million dollars go easily.*

CHAPTER FOURTEEN

Jim Calhoun had just gotten off the phone after formally requesting to take the next two weeks off. He'd used family issues as the reason and pretended to be upset. His supervisor had wished him well and told him to take as much time as he needed. Then he placed another call. "Prepare to copy."

"Go ahead," the voice replied.

"Get the Learjet fueled and loaded. Untraceable weapons, secure communications, and the proper paperwork for secured entry into the Bahamas."

"Copy. What else?"

"There must be no mistakes and no connection with the operation. Whatever it costs to keep this quiet, I'm willing to pay."

"Copy. Any other resources you think will be helpful?"

"Not unless you can find Thomas."

"I haven't heard from him. No request for a fund transfer."

"That's what I figured."

Calhoun assumed Thomas was either AWOL, dead or captured. The sniper knew nothing to connect the operation to Calhoun. But, if he could confirm

Thomas had been captured, he'd make sure the mercenary was killed.

"Do you need assistance?" asked the voice.

"This could get ugly if we don't locate him soon. Prepare my other resources for quick departure. If things get hot, I'll shut everything down. We won't do business again. Ever." Calhoun's voice reflected his anger.

"You've had a good run, sir. Once everything's taken care of here, I might be useful in the field."

Calhoun hesitated. "I agree. You'll come along to fly us out of the hot zone when it's over."

"Got it. I'll be ready for departure at zero dark five tomorrow."

Calhoun sighed. "Zero dark five it is. Change the location to the alternate point B for departure."

"Roger that."

Calhoun knew he didn't have to tell his son how important this operation was. No one even knew about his son's existence. The kid was the product of a liaison with a woman on Andros Island who had died in childbirth. He had paid anonymously to have the boy raised by a local family there, and only contacted the kid when he was grown.

The Coast Guard commander began to plan how they'd retrieve the hundred million dollar cargo without being apprehended so they could spend the rest of their lives in complete luxury.

CHAPTER FIFTEEN

As they waited for the police to arrive, Roger said, "We should let them know we found this guy's gear including the GPS with the coordinates for the boat."

Petersen shook his head. "They might get pissed that we went through their crime scene. No cop likes that."

Dix, who'd rejoined them after his call, made another suggestion. "I think we should lead them to the coordinates. Roger can remind them the boat Sean and Preston were on hasn't been found. They may decide to check the GPS if we give it to them."

"You think we should let them find the boat and all the cocaine?" asked Roger.

Petersen nodded and Dix said, "Yes. It makes sense to let them have the credit for locating the boat. They have the equipment to raise it. Besides, it's really their case."

"Yes, but their storage yard is burglarized all the time. Local kids climb over the fence and take what they want." Roger threw up his hands.

Dix heard the sirens growing louder. "You want to hear what I'm thinking? We have a lot of good information about this Caller guy, but not much to nail him with. Even if we knew who he was, I'm not sure we'd be able to get a search warrant or arrest warrant for him."

"What about a trap?" suggested Petersen.

"Exactly. If the storage facility isn't secure, we could work with the locals, and maybe the Coast Guard and U.S. Navy, to set a trap. Maybe the Coast Guard would even lend us Jim Calhoun for the investigation."

As he finished his statement, two police vans skidded to a stop in front of the house. Roger pointed them to the body. Everyone had their hands in the air. A senior officer rushed to the body and quickly pronounced Thomas dead.

Another officer took the rifle near Roger's feet and began to question him while others converged on the area around the body. Dix recognized one of the officers as one he had seen at the airport when he arrived on the island. A few minutes later, the officer's voice rang out. "What the hell was a sniper doing here on Andros?" His voice carried, so the rest of the cops stopped what they were doing. He pointed at Dix and Petersen. "And why are these guys here?"

Dix and Petersen looked at each other and shrugged.

Roger spoke. "I invited these two fishermen to try my special rolls." Then he pointed to the sniper's belongings he'd taken from the chest pockets. "I took that stuff out after he was dead."

The officer looked angry. "Why'd you do that?"

Roger remained cool. "I started CPR on him, but it didn't work. I had to take the stuff out to do the compressions."

Dix thought, *good call, Roger.*

"Then your prints will be on the items, correct?

"Yes."

One of the other guys stepped forward and pointed at the three men. "Do you want me to print all of them?"

The senior officer said, "That won't be necessary." He pointed at Roger. "I booked him when he was a kid after he had a little too much to drink one night. His prints are already on file."

For the next hour or so, Roger, Dix, and Petersen skillfully directed the officers to the information they'd already learned. The local guys required little prompting and quickly connected Thomas to the deaths of Sean and Preston.

The officers told everyone at Roger's house not to leave the island, and the lead officer gave Petersen and Dix his business card. "You guys think of anything we missed, don't hesitate to call me."

Dix and Petersen looked sincere and said in unison, "You bet." The local officers left as they wheeled Thomas's body to the van. Everyone except Dix went inside Roger's home.

CHAPTER SIXTEEN

Dix dialed the number for Sergeant Michael Pierce, but as it rang, he heard the distinctive tone telling him he had an incoming call. He figured since he'd kept his sergeant in the dark this long, a few more minutes wouldn't make much difference.

He answered the incoming call from Snead. "Boy, you clear to copy some information?"

"Absolutely. What have you got?"

"Info on the boat. It was made in Florida and registered to Jackie Spears *after* she was found dead. It's been registered in Jamaica, the Bahamas, and even Columbia. Aliases for different dead people were used for each registration in each country. Now, how do you like them facts?"

Dix grunted. "This Caller guy's good. He's left no traces to anyone alive. Where were the tags sent?"

"I checked. People can go to the DMV to pick up the decals and stickers."

Dix thought for a moment. "Don't those places have cameras?"

"Yep, at least the one here does. I'm not sure how my sources got the intel, but they said a white male adult picked up the decals and registration information for the speedboat you're after. They said he looked at the cameras several times and grinned."

"I wonder what that means."

"Well, here's where it gets real interesting. My guys tried to find the man through all available databases. Even used some facial recognition software. They got nothing. According to these guys, the smiling man doesn't exist."

"Jesus. I wonder if he's the Caller." Dix felt himself get a little excited.

"I wondered myself. The guy on the surveillance tapes was about thirty. How would he have the resources to pull this stuff off?"

"Maybe he works for the Caller." *Man, this is getting complicated.*

"Some vacation."

Snead chuckled. "You and that pile of horse manure you keep stompin' your big boots in."

"Go ahead. Rub it in." Dix was laughing too.

"You might want to know I've got certified copies of the registration for the boat. Since it's currently registered out of Florida, I think you could make a case it belongs to the Miami-Dade Police Department."

"But it's in the Bahamas right now." Dix thought Snead had a point, but how could Miami-Dade claim it?

"Seems to me, whoever retrieves the boat could file a claim on it."

Dix considered Snead's point and decided it was way beyond time to report the situation to Sergeant Pierce.

Snead cleared his throat. "Since you're not saying anything, I'm guessing you're thinking about what I just said. I figured you'd want this case for yourself."

"I do, but I really want to catch the Caller. And I think this one belongs to the Bahamians."

"Don't know if guys that good get caught. You've been around long enough to know we usually only catch the ones who're dumber than dirt."

"I know, but if we let the Bahamians get the boat and store it, the guy just might come looking for it." Dix sounded hopeful.

"Or he might just send more mercenaries."

"Good point," Dix said. "But I think he'll come himself.

It's too big a haul not to."

Snead ran scenarios that could help Dix. "He may show up to check on his sniper. He'll want him pushin' up daisies. What about calling the feds for extra help?"

"Yes. I figure between the AWOL sniper and the sunken load, our guy won't trust anyone else. We're hoping the Bahamian cops will make contact with the Coast Guard, at least."

"Before you're up to your neck in muck, call up Sergeant Pierce and drop the bomb on him."

Dix cringed. "That was my plan. Thanks for everything."

"Not a problem. Keep me in the loop." The line went dead.

Dix walked back to Roger's house and shared the information he'd received from Snead with the others. Before he got caught up in small talk, he decided he'd waited long enough to talk to Sergeant Pierce.

CHAPTER SEVENTEEN

Dix called Pierce's number again. This time he was determined to talk to him before he encountered more distractions. However, the call rolled to voicemail, so Dix left a message.

Five minutes later, his phone rang.

Even before Dix could answer, he heard his boss's voice. "Pierce here. What's up?"

"Sergeant Pierce. Thanks for calling back. You know how Petersen seems to be a shit magnet?"

Pierce laughed. "Don't tell me you guys are in jail. That would make my day, maybe the whole year. Hell, probably my entire career."

Dix cleared his throat and tried to decide how to approach the subject. "I wish it was that easy. You know I wouldn't call you for that."

"Then what the hell is it? We're actually working here while you and Petersen lie in the sun. I don't want to hear how great your trip is."

"This won't take long, and it can't wait." Dix was prepared for his boss to erupt.

"Damn it. It's bad, isn't it?"

"I'll give you the condensed version. We have a vessel last registered in Miami, Florida, that we think was headed to Miami before it was sunk. Both people on board were murdered. The boat is loaded with cocaine with a street value in excess of one hundred million dollars. A hired mercenary sniper, named M. A. Thomas, gave us information about the guy running the entire operation, a male adult known locally only as the Caller..."

"Hold on!" Pierce slammed the horn is his car, "Hey, get the hell out of the way."

Dix laughed out loud.

"Okay, continue with this crazy story," said Pierce.

"The sniper also confessed to the murders. He escaped and opened fire on the home where he'd been detained. The homeowner killed him before he could be turned over to the local police. They were called, and we told them most of what we knew. They have the coordinates for the speedboat and plan to bring it up and store it, but the facility they use isn't secure. With your permission, Petersen and I would like to be involved at this end. Maybe Miami-Dade can get this guy."

Pierce shook his head. "Are you kidding me? You guys are on vacation in the Bahamas and you want the department's help with a drug case you just happened to stumble into?"

"Sarge, this case just might cinch your promotion to lieutenant, and the whole unit might get a commendation. Maybe the whole department.

Think of the great publicity. We might need the help of the Coast Guard and whoever else you think would be useful."

Pierce covered the microphone on his phone, and Dix heard garbled conversation before the sergeant spoke again. "Here's what we'll do. I'll call the captain. You handle things on your end. I'll notify the Coast Guard and U.S. Navy, and open a line of communication with the Bahamians. We do this right, and we got a shot of coming out as heroes. That is, as long as you two don't mess it up."

"Okay, Sarge. Obviously, if I learn anything new, I'll let you know."

Pierce grunted. "One more thing. You guys catch any fish? What do they call them, bones or something?"

Dix chuckled. "Yeah, one. They're called bonefish. Some of the locals call them gray ghosts."

"You get this deal done, and I just might approve your vacation request for next year."

Dix laughed as Pierce hung up.

It had gone better than he'd thought. *Now to get on with solving the case.*

CHAPTER EIGHTEEN

Snead fired up his computer, poured a tall cup of black coffee, and sent some requests to friends in other agencies. Then he waited. Soon the replies started. He waded through the suggestions and did his own follow-ups. Roughly three hours into it, he caught a break. According to his research, the speedboat was custom built in 2000, not 2007, and the buyer used an electronic fund transfer to purchase it.

The wire transfer was a mistake. One of Snead's contact's skills was the ability to decipher worms, codes, and language intended to send interested parties in the wrong direction. Information embedded in the data was left behind. The transaction traced back to a Dell computer purchased by the Coast Guard. His heart nearly stopped.

"Check again."

His contact replied, "There's no mistake."

"Thanks. See if you can get the exact date and time of the transaction."

"Will do."

Snead hung up. He was starting to think someone in the Coast Guard could be involved in the mess Dix and Petersen were in.

If he was lucky, he might be able to narrow down the number of people who could have made the transaction.

And he hoped he'd find the Caller.

He refreshed his coffee, popped a Hot Pockets in the microwave and began to make more calls. Many people owed him favors, and he intended to collect every last one of them.

CHAPTER NINETEEN

As the Bahamians worked with the Royal Netherlands Navy to raise the *Gray Ghost*, local fishermen watched from their boats. They were ordered to stay a long distance away from the effort.

As the boat was slowly lifted to the surface, assisted by massive airbags, a Coast Guard UAV flew overhead documenting the scene. One of the Bahamian divers looked up, caught a glimpse of the object, and pointed it out. The crew stopped what they were doing and watched the expensive toy fly away, make a large circle back, and fly overhead again at a high rate of speed.

Thousands of bubbles broke the surface as the speedboat came up. The vessel was about three feet from the surface when an air bag along the stern exploded. Two quick-thinking divers grabbed huge orange buoys and leaped into the water. They attempted to get a rope around the stern to keep the boat afloat. It worked. The boat stayed in position long enough to work another airbag under the stern. About that time, the lead officer ordered the locals to leave in order to create a straight path for the recovered boat to the main dock.

Once the boat was secured on the flat barge, the cocaine was placed in the locked compartments of the other police boats. When all was ready, the convoy set a course to the main boat ramp. Local boats stayed well behind the convoy as a Coast Guard and Royal Navy cruiser escorted the speedboat. A tugboat ran alongside to assist.

Roughly four hours later, two Royal Bahamian vessels loaded with cocaine and the speedboat arrived at the main dock. The Yukon Denali, which had originally towed the boat, and the custom trailer hitched to it already sat waiting. Twelve armed officers guarded the scene and oversaw the process.

Another two hours passed before the damaged boat was finally onto the custom trailer. Then, escorted by what seemed like every police service vehicle on the island, the boat was towed to the storage yard, which doubled as the police warehouse.

Dix and Petersen waited as the boat and trailer were secured in the warehouse. They observed as local officers began to file out of their vehicles and take up defensive positions around the warehouse.

One of the officers, Prescott, according to his badge, said, "Won't they laugh when they find out the dope ain't in the boat?"

"What the hell are you talking about? Where the hell's the dope?" Dix yelled.

The officer explained that they'd moved the cocaine into their secured police boats to ensure they wouldn't lose the drugs. These boats were still at the main dock.

Dix frantically grabbed the officer's radio from his shirt and yelled, "All units, all units, code three to the dock. I repeat, code three to the docks."

"I can't believe you did that. Every officer in the area is here. You left a huge shipment of drugs unguarded back at the marina?" Dix said.

Dix and Petersen jumped into the car they'd borrowed from Roger.

The detectives raced back to the dock, followed by the local officers. Petersen looked through binoculars. "I can see the boats, I count two. There's no one around them. Punch it!"

The speeding vehicles came to a halt, and everyone ran to the police boats moored in their slips. One by one, they were checked, and the contents accounted for. Each still contained the packages of cocaine. Petersen and Dix exchanged glances.

Dix demanded to speak to the officer in charge (OIC). No one responded. He took several deep breaths and decided their own department could deal with the incompetence.

"We all make mistakes, but this cannot happen again. Double check, then triple check everything you do from here on out. I won't tell your boss about this if you don't." Dix addressed the officers at the scene, who were embarrassed but expressed their appreciation for how he had handled it.

Dix and Petersen decided to split up, one in each police van, as the cocaine was taken from the marina to the warehouse. When they arrived at the warehouse, they assisted as the officers unloaded the cocaine into large, black duffel bags and placed them in secured storage lockers next to the speedboat. Dix shook his head and rubbed his chin. He looked at Petersen, who rolled his eyes at him. *This just gets worse by the minute*, thought Dix.

CHAPTER TWENTY

At four in the morning, Calhoun was awakened by a constant chirping of his cell phone. He'd been dreaming of an exotic island with beautiful women. *Whoever this is better have a good reason for waking me.*

He rolled out of bed, retrieved the device, and accepted the data link to the flashing message. Then he activated the speaker function of his smart phone.

"UAV images you must see," a voice said.

He moved the mouse attached to his laptop to get it to start processing and saw a message with an attachment in his inbox. He double checked the source of the message to confirm it came from his son's secure, wireless link. Calhoun double clicked the paperclip representing an attachment, and the computer downloaded a video. He clicked play on the media player.

The first images showed several small boats and a larger one in the water.

The narrator spoke. "That video was taken off the northern end of Andros Island."

Calhoun wasn't impressed. It didn't matter if they knew about the drugs because he didn't have to worry about getting the boat up by himself. As the

UAV got closer to the boats, his computer froze and then shut down. *What the hell is this?*

He turned his laptop back on and found the link to gain access to the video again. Calhoun grinned as the video came in crystal clear, and he saw the speedboat he wanted just beneath the surface. He watched the boat almost slip away as an airbag burst, but two divers jumped in to save it. Images from the UAV showed the cocaine being unloaded from *Gray Ghost* and placed in police vessels. The UAV quickly left the area once the boats appeared headed for the journey to the dock.

Calhoun chuckled. The poor bastards have no idea what they're doing.

Eventually, he'd hoped they'd store the cocaine somewhere easy to access. He planned to make his move in about three days. Calhoun knew law enforcement tactics. He'd even written about them and figured the first few days the local officers would guard the storage facility aggressively. When nothing happened, they'd begin to let their guard down. That's when he and his son would wait for the cocaine to be delivered to them on the tarmac. Calhoun planned to use an elite Coast Guard unit, known as a DOG Unit, to storm the facility, grab the cocaine, and be gone before anyone knew what happened.

CHAPTER TWENTY ONE

Sergeant Pierce informed his guys that operations were over. "Take the rest of the day off. Report at zero seven hundred hours tomorrow."

Some of the men grumbled.

"Dix and Petersen stumbled onto a major drug operation while they were supposed to be on vacation in the Bahamas. Go home and rest. Tomorrow could be rough." Pierce watched his men leave, then dialed the narcotics lieutenant and filled him in on the details. Once that was done, Pierce relaxed some but still had calls to make.

He notified the other agencies potentially involved in the operation in the U.S. When he finished the last call, he remembered he had a date night with his wife. They had reservations at a classy restaurant and tickets for a play for the following evening to celebrate their anniversary. He probably wasn't going to be available for that special night, so he made some calls to see if he could come up with a backup plan. Then he dialed his home number.

Before he could utter a word, his wife said, "Let me guess. Another high priority case, right?"

"Sorry, honey, but I can make it work. I changed our plans to tonight. Are you game?"

"You did what? How? It took two months to get the dinner reservations."

"Don't ask. Just get dressed and be ready for an enjoyable night." Pierce loved his wife more than anything and wanted to make her feel special.

As he jumped into his truck, he remembered he hadn't called his old friend, Jim Calhoun, to see if he knew anything about the circus happening in the Bahamas. He figured if they had any shot at catching the bad guy, they'd need Jim's expertise and resources.

Pierce dialed Calhoun's cell number. It went straight to voicemail. He thought it odd since he teased Jim often that he was attached at the hip to his cell phone.

He left a message. "Jim, Mike Pierce here. Call me. I think I'm gonna need your help."

Then after he had hung up, he realized he'd forgotten flowers for his wife. Fortunately, there was a florist on the way home. A dozen roses was a good start to a great evening.

CHAPTER TWENTY-TWO

Dix and Petersen began assessing their options at the police warehouse. Wilfred had arrived to join them.

"Since we're here, we ought to look for vantage points where we can observe the boat. I figure the Coast Guard will send that cutter we saw yesterday, and maybe the helicopter we saw too," Dix said.

Petersen nodded. "Yeah, if they get here in time. Our navy might send some help, and the local one may assign some equipment and personnel too. But it has to happen in a hurry."

Dix nodded. "The Caller might slip through if he's affiliated with one of the agencies involved. I don't want to believe it, but how else has he been able to remain undetected for so long?"

Petersen raised an eyebrow. "Do you really think it's a possibility?"

"Absolutely. I can't explain how else he could have been so successful and knowledgeable about how things work unless he was trained by the people he's taking advantage of. His understanding of the operations of local law enforcement and drug interdiction is well beyond what ordinary people would know. No one has a clue who he is, and he's remained untraceable, even by MIT boys. Gotta have special clearance."

Petersen turned to Wilfred. "You said you know some of the people on the island who might have information about the Caller. Why don't you collect Bubba and Roger and see what you can come up with?" He handed Wilfred a business card from his wallet. "Here's my cell number. Call me if you find out anything."

"Okay. I can think of a couple of guys to ask." Wilfred took the keys to Roger's car, got in, and drove away.

Dix called Roger. "Wilfred is on his way with your car. We've asked him to take you and Bubba to see if you guys can find out anything more about the Caller."

Roger replied, "Sounds like a plan."

Dix continued, "And I need a favor. Petersen and I need guns. You have a few lying around we can use?"

"Certainly. I'll grab two and get them to you ASAP."

Dix was curious how exactly Roger had so many weapons. "Roger, I have to ask, where do you get all the weapons?"

"Oh, I'm just a gun nut. Always been around them, and I collect."

Something in Roger's voice made Dix suspect it was a lie, but Roger didn't provide any more information.

Dix suspected things were about to get real interesting on the island and felt he and Petersen should be armed, just in case. "Thanks. We'll let you know if we need them. Wilfred should arrive in a few minutes."

"I'll be ready."

Dix hung up and grimaced at Petersen. "We pissed away our fishing trip to help a couple guys. Now, we're too deep to pull out. I'd be lying if I said I didn't want to catch this jackass, but I don't want to die here unarmed."

Petersen nodded. "Amen, buddy. Let's canvass the area on foot. The OIC is near the gate."

After determining a few weak places susceptible to a breach, Dix and Petersen found the officer in charge.

Dix shook his hand. "We've looked around, and there might be some spots where someone could get in fairly easily. Also, there's a few spots where your people can keep a look out without being detected easily."

"Yes, I have been considering that very thing," said the OIC.

"Good. Then we're all working on the same plan. I'd like to discuss where surveillance equipment could be placed when you have the time. What are your thoughts?"

"Tomorrow morning might be best," the OIC replied. Dix was anxious to get some rest and set the trap.

"Good. Tomorrow it is. Oh, and would it be possible to borrow some firearms from your department while we're here? We might need protection."

The OIC frowned. "Unfortunately, that might prove to be difficult. Rules and regulations, you know. The chief doesn't want to make any exceptions, no matter how big this case is."

Dix looked at Petersen. "We understand. We have strict rules in Miami, too. We're officers, though. You sure he won't change his mind?" The OIC shook his head and gave a look like don't ask again.

Petersen stepped forward. "Are there any aerial photos of this facility?"

The OIC hesitated. "I might be able to locate something."

"Good. That would be helpful. Thank you so much. Let us know what we can do to be of assistance. After all, it's your case."

"I certainly shall. You have my deepest thanks for your contributions so far."

Dix thought for a second that the OIC was going to salute Petersen, but he just nodded and walked away.

"Good thing I already asked Roger for weapons. I was afraid we'd get the official answer in the negative. Do you think Roger might also have some spare body armor and a few flash-bang grenades?"

Petersen chuckled. "From the way his boys were armed, he probably has a whole arsenal."

Dix frowned. "We should get maps and flight plans for all small aircraft entering Bahamian air space."

Petersen hadn't considered that. "You think this guy is coming by plane?"

"He's good, but not good enough to get past all the agency ships, which should arrive soon. I don't think he'll be on one of them."

Petersen leaned against the warehouse wall and ran his hands through his hair. "Man, I'm beat, how about you?"

"I'm tired, but let's talk this out before we turn in."

Petersen rolled his eyes. "Okay, what else you thinking?"

"Every incoming vessel will be stopped and may be boarded at sea. Everyone will be questioned. My guess is he'll come in on a small plane and look like every other arriving tourist." Petersen nodded.

"We might also need a laptop, night vision goggles, and camouflage gear. I'll see if Pierce will send those overnight."

Petersen shook his head. "That stuff won't make it in time. We'll have to improvise, buddy."

Dix moved beyond the comment. "Every way on and off this island must be monitored. I'm not sure we have the bodies to cover it all."

Petersen nodded. "Do you think the Caller has someone on his payroll working for the Royal Bahamian Police Force?"

"I guess corrupt cops can be found in any agency." *Great question. He's learning.*

"This is the peak fly fishing season. Planes will be landing every hour. Surveillance at the airport will be difficult." Petersen rubbed his chin.

Dix agreed. "We'll just have to take it one plane at a time.

Come on, we need to get some work done."

Dix and Petersen requested two local officers to accompany them as they further scouted the area around the warehouse. They walked the vicinity and considered access points, vantage points, and exit routes.

Noting a lot of deficiencies, Dix noted, "Whoever comes after the narcotics knows the place will be guarded. There's sure to be a confrontation. Our people have to be able to get in and out safely."

"How do you think they'll try to get the drugs out?" one of the Bahamian officers asked Dix.

He thought for a moment. "They'd need a large cargo van or maybe an armored truck to get into the warehouse. Probably three minutes to load the cocaine, depending how many men show up, then leave as fast as they can."

The officer said, "There are plenty of vans on the island because of the dive shops and lodges, but I don't think any are armored."

Petersen shook his head. "It would take too long to unload the dope from the duffel bags and put it in another vehicle. They may send more guys just to make sure they can lift the bags quickly. Then we're only talking about thirty to forty seconds until they'd be able to leave."

Dix caught himself chewing on his nails. "Good thought. Maybe we should take the dope out of the bags and put it back in the boat the way it was found."

Some of the officers nodded, others shook their heads.

Petersen held up a hand. "The bad guy is going to know the jig is up since we raised the boat. He'd know officers would take the cocaine out to determine how much was there, to weigh it, photograph it, and book it."

"So if we put it back in the boat, the Caller would surely know he'd be walking into a trap," said Dix.

A local officer chimed in. "If the cocaine is in the speedboat, whoever comes to grab it could tow it straight to the airport. From there, they could load the cocaine onto a plane, and be gone for good."

Dix dismissed the idea with a wave of his hand. "That would take too long, plus it doesn't make sense based on what Petersen said."

Petersen looked thoughtful. "Or they could put the duffel bags into a helicopter and leave even more quickly."

Dix turned to the local guys. "Besides Mangrove Cay, how many other places are there on the island flat and clear enough to land a small plane or helicopter and get it off the ground again?"

A Bahamian officer who'd remained quiet until now replied, "Opposite ends of the island. Two other fields, one on the north end of the island and the other is to the south."

Petersen turned to him. "I don't know a lot about helicopters, but I bet a skilled pilot could get one down just east of the storage unit and back in the air in a few minutes." Dix nodded. "You're right. We better make sure the Coast Guard's Stingray choppers are close by and ready for an aerial intercept. We should also see if the navy has a few jets they could scramble if things get hot."

One of the local officers looked at the other, then back at Dix. "You guys really think someone would be dumb enough to try to get this cocaine? I know it's worth a lot, but if the guy is as smart as you think, wouldn't he realize we'd set a trap?"

Dix laughed. "A hundred million dollars makes sane people crazy. Given what we know about the mastermind you guys named the Caller, he is cocky and arrogant enough to think he could pull this off. He's been able to get everything he's wanted for a long time. We're pretty sure he won't let this haul get away."

Petersen added, "Besides, the guy thinks he's untouchable, and he loves outsmarting the authorities. This haul is big enough, he might even decide to retire."

Several more Royal Bahamian Police Force guys strolled toward them. One carried what appeared to be folded maps.

They approached but didn't acknowledge Dix or Petersen. *That's strange.*

The local officers opened the schematics on the hood of a cruiser and began pointing at weaknesses or potential routes in or out of the facility. They formed a half-circle, essentially shielding Dix and Petersen from their discussion.

Dix was miffed and about to say something when the OIC walked up. "What the hell are you men doing? Dix and Petersen are Miami narcotics detectives working with us. Move over and let them see what you have."

The men separated to allow Dix and Petersen to join their circle.

Something isn't right here.

The schematics showed the area in and around the storage unit. After some discussion, the group identified two locations difficult to fortify and defend. They walked to each area to closely examine how the Caller, or his men, could break through their defenses.

Petersen looked to the side and nudged Dix. "With all the attention we've been giving this place, seems we've attracted a following."

Dix followed Petersen's gaze and noticed they were being observed by several locals. "We're going to spend a little more time here and then beat feet."

"Great, the sooner we leave, the sooner I can get a beer." Petersen licked his lips. "By now, everyone probably knows something was recovered from the speedboat and transported under heavy guard to the warehouse. You know how it is, Petersen, people get curious."

Dix decided they could spend all night at the storage unit, but frankly he was finished strategizing. He was excited as the locals discussed installing surveillance cameras and said they'd handle most of the operational tasks for the pending takedown. However, if he felt they were making poor decisions, he'd jump in and get the issue resolved.

Turning to the others, Dix spoke again. "Everyone's worked hard today. You guys up for some cold beer and grub?"

One of the officers looked confused. "What's grub?"

Petersen and Dix chuckled. Dix answered, "Back home it's another name for food. You guys ready to eat?"

The Bahamians laughed and nodded.

Then Dix realized he had no idea where to go. "You guys got any suggestions? I'll buy."

The men grinned. The Florida cops should have known they go to the most expensive joint on Andros Island.

CHAPTER TWENTY-THREE

Given the circumstances, Calhoun was pleased with how things were developing. The cocaine he'd stolen from his Columbian competitor had been located.

Calhoun had arranged for a duplicate speed boat with the name *Gray Ghost* for it to arrive at the exact location where the original load was supposed to have been delivered at the port of Miami. The boat was even loaded with kilos of baking soda to make it look authentic. In doing so, Calhoun hoped it would take his competitor a few days to figure out what actually happened. By then, it would be too late.

A source used by Calhoun gave him an update. The Bahamian Government had brought the cocaine up from the ocean floor, packaged it in duffel bags, and stored it in a lousy facility. The duffel bags containing the cocaine were in a locked cabinet next to the boat. Calhoun figured he could easily outsmart the local officers. He had a few tricks up his sleeve to ensure he'd maintain the upper hand.

The biggest advantage he had was having two Bahamian officers on his payroll. They regularly kept him advised of everything the local officers knew. However, neither of them had checked in for two hours. Calhoun figured they were making preparations for his arrival.

For several years, these two men had been instrumental in his operations. *Maybe I should have paid them more.* When the sniper failed, he'd been angry. Now the situation seemed under complete control, his control. He laughed because he planned to orchestrate the entire operation from thirty thousand feet in the air.

He met his son at the agreed upon location. Personally checking to be sure the jet was fueled and loaded, he had left nothing to chance.

Calhoun watched his son get out of the Yukon Denali. He felt enormous pride. Junior was intellectually and physically gifted, but above all, he was respectful of his father. Calhoun put a hand on the young man's shoulder. "Son, I'm pulling the plug on this whole operation after this job. We will have enough money stored around the globe to live extremely well."

He could see the disappointment on the young man's face. "I went to college for you. I joined the military for you. I completed Special Ops training for you. I've even killed for you. I did it because I thought I'd take over when you were too old to run the show."

"I'm willing to discuss this with you after we're done in the Bahamas. Until then, we drop it."

When his son was born, after he'd lost his precious daughter, Jackie, he promised he'd protect him better than Jackie. Now he wondered if keeping him so sheltered had been a mistake.

"Okay. I'll focus on this mission, and I'll do what is necessary to make it successful. But I won't forget about this."

"All right, son.   Let's get to Andros and retrieve some cocaine. Afterward, we'll discuss this over champagne."

Junior nodded.

Calhoun began mentally preparing for the operation. "Good. Confirm the sniper rifles are packed."

"Check."

"And the flash-bang grenades?"

"Check."

"Did you remember the less-than-lethal shotgun?"

"Check."

"Fantastic. Are we good?" Calhoun's son paused.

"For now."

They boarded a G5 jet Calhoun had seized for the Coast Guard. The look on the guy's face, when he saw Calhoun take the jet, had been priceless. Junior fired up the twin jet engines. For the first time in a long, long while, Calhoun focused on family matters as he sat in the cockpit. In the back of his mind, he thought it might be catastrophic to think about family instead of the operation.

CHAPTER TWENTY-FOUR

Suzie whispered in her husband's ear, "Someone's here to see you about Sean and Preston."

Martin excused himself from their guests, left the main dining room, and went outside. Standing near the lodge entrance was a woman he'd seen around town over the years. She was shaking and sobbing uncontrollably.

Martin took her hand.

She looked up and pressed a tissue to her eyes. "I may have information about Preston and Sean. I don't want to go to the police because I don't trust them. I know they worked for the Caller. Preston said I could trust you. He told me if anything ever happened to him, I should tell you."

"You did the right thing. I loved Preston and Sean like brothers. You can trust me."

She shook. "I'm afraid the Caller will kill me, too if he finds out I told you."

Martin put an arm around her. "The Caller is currently being hunted, but no one knows who he is."

She whispered, "Preston said he thought the Caller was a white man, who works for the Coast Guard."

Martin was stunned. "What would make him think that?"

"He mentioned something about a UAV. He said they're Coast Guard drone planes which patrol the ocean looking for drug runners. He said they were all over the Caribbean, but when he and Sean made a run, they were never around. Since they never saw one and the Caller made all of their arrangements, Preston thought the Caller knew when they were flying. Preston assumed the Caller worked for the Coast Guard because no one else would know about the UAVs."

Martin nodded. "Did Preston tell you anything else?"

She began to cry again, and Martin stepped back. When she regained her composure, she said, "Preston asked some people about how the Coast Guard operates, you know, how decisions are made and who makes them. He found out the UAVs are experimental. Only the highest ranking officers would know when and where they were in use."

Martin scratched his head. "Did he indicate who he thought the Caller might be?"

"Not that I know of. He might have told Sean, but not me."

Martin patted her hand. "This is very helpful. You did the right thing. I know you're scared, but we have to try to stop this man before he hurts anyone else. Would you be willing to talk to some friends of mine? They can be trusted. They're trying to figure this out."

She pulled her hand away and looked nervous. "Are they policemen?"

"Yes, but not from the island. They're my guests who happen to be narcotic detectives from Miami. They've been investigating Sean and Preston's murders."

She hesitated. "Okay, but I don't want anyone else to know about it."

Martin grabbed his cell phone and dialed Dix's number.

The call went to voicemail.

"Dix, call me back immediately. I have information about the Caller. He's a high-ranking official with the Coast Guard. I'll explain later."

Martin turned to the woman. "Go home. I'll be in touch."

As soon as she left, Martin tracked Suzie down. "Come on. I need to go into town to find Dix and Petersen. Can you drive me?" She grabbed her keys. "Of course, baby."

As they got into the car, Martin told her to try Hank's first.

CHAPTER TWENTY-FIVE

Snead finished his Hot Pockets and coffee. He decided to leave the computer search to his MIT friends, and instead, hit the streets looking for his old CIs. He put a Springfield XD three-inch subcompact pistol on his hip before he left. *You never know when you will need a weapon.*

He drove to the very tough streets of Liberty City, an impoverished neighborhood within the Miami city limits. More than eighty percent of all drug-related activity originated there. He took a risk being seen since he was both white and an ex-cop.

Tonight, however, he needed the people of the streets to help him assist Dix. They'd sometimes talk to him because they thought he might be a customer looking to purchase drugs.

Eventually, he ran into two prostitutes shooting heroin in an alley.

They looked up when they saw him. "Hey, you a narc?" asked one.

The other slid over and put her arm through his. "Oh, he just wants a twofer for a dime, don't you, sweetie."

Snead shook his head and pulled his arm from hers. "I just want answers."

"Well, we're plum out." They went back to shooting up. He gave up trying to be rational with the two women.

They were of no help and would be even less as soon as the heroin entered their bloodstream.

Snead walked down the street until he got to the intersection of A Street and Third Avenue. A large group of men knelt huddled close together. It looked as if they were playing craps since they had gathered in a circle throwing what looked like dice.

One of them glanced up and pointed at Snead. Several of the men ran away on foot. *Probably have warrants*. The rest went back to their game and dismissed his presence. He continued to the corner to see if he knew any of those who had remained.

As he got about ten feet from the group he heard, "Hey, Sarge, what's up?"

Snead quickly looked to his left and saw several men standing in the shadows of a burned-out building. *Dammit, how did I miss them?*

He recognized all of them. At one time or another, he had arrested either them or their older relatives.

Two left the shadows and approached. Tyrone Holmes offered his hand to shake. Snead took it.

Holmes said, "Man, how the hell are you? It's been a while. Last time I saw you, you were wearing BDUs and chasing my nephew."

Snead smiled. "I recall that incident vaguely. Your nephew was so fast he ran through the perimeter, made it to his aunt's house, and called you."

"If he hadn't hurt my sister trying to steal her car, I wouldn't have called you."

"I remember. You told us where to find him. We did the rest."

Tyrone nodded. "I talked to him last week in jail. He's okay. Said he wants to get a real job when he gets out and buy his aunt a new car for wrecking hers in the high-speed chase. He was always a good kid when he wasn't high."

Holmes smiled. "Most of the people out here are. How's your wife?"

"She's good. She got promoted to vice principal at the high school. She sure loves kids." Snead paused and looked Holmes in the eye. "Speaking of kids, what's happening with yours?"

"My son's the starting quarterback on junior varsity, and my daughter's still taking dance and acting classes." He patted Snead on the shoulder. "Thanks for helping me to get my priorities straight."

Snead smiled. "I just gave you a break. You took advantage of it and got clean. The credit goes to you, my friend."

Holmes smiled, and then grew serious. "Let's get to business. What brings you out this way?"

Snead took a deep breath. "A long time ago, when you and I were much younger, most of the dealers out here were supplied by one guy. No one ever cared who he was as long as the dope made it in their hands. Everyone assumed he was a Columbian, but I think he might have been from the United States."

Holmes shook his head. "Be straight. Are you looking for a specific dealer or the word on the street?"

"At this point, any information would help. You remember Dix and Petersen? They're still working as narcs." Holmes nodded.

Snead gave some information about the case to Holmes. Not all of it, but enough to see if it would jog his memory. He closed with the fact about the locals tagging the main guy as the Caller.

Holmes appeared shocked. "Fifteen years ago, I did some business with a guy who always worked over the phone. I met him once, but he used me a few times to distribute cocaine. The guy didn't want to meet in person, but we had a very large deal in the works. I insisted. Since I had the cash, he finally agreed."

Holmes hesitated, looked around, and then continued. "I went by myself, but my crew was nearby waiting for a signal. The guy showed up with two other goons. The dudes working for the supplier frisked me and found my snub-nosed .38 Special. They took it and stood on both sides of me."

Snead moved closer. "So what happened?"

Holmes shrugged. "It came down fast. I showed him the cash. He showed me the cocaine. I checked the goods and we went our separate ways. I never met him again."

Snead's interest was piqued. "Do you remember anything about the guy?"

"Ah, man, I don't know. That was a long time ago."

Snead played another card. "I think Dix and Petersen are in danger. I'm trying to help them. Anything at all will help."

Holmes closed his eyes for what seemed to Snead like five minutes. "Well, the guy was white, middle-aged, maybe thirty at the time. He spoke English with a slight southern accent. The two thugs with him had short haircuts and were in great shape. I sure didn't want to mess with them."

Holmes stopped for a minute. "Oh, I think they might have been packing Colt .45 caliber sidearms. The guy making the decisions seemed new to the dope business. He didn't know the language we used, and he was real jumpy. He was about your height, maybe six foot. Built like you, too, athletic with a long torso."

Snead was excited. "Was anyone dumb enough to let a name slip?"

"Maybe, but I don't remember much of what they said."

Snead continued. "When you think of the stereotypical military man, what do you think of?"

"I'd say white guys with short hair, muscular, and kind of cocky. Sort of like the guys I saw that night."

Snead gave up another piece of the puzzle. "Dix thinks the Caller may have ties with the navy or Coast Guard."

Holmes's eyes grew big.

Their conversation was cut short by a hail of gunfire followed by mass confusion. A Chevy Impala with chrome rims slowly rolled by, and neither Snead nor Holmes had seen it. Two passengers began firing on the group playing craps. Automatic rifle rounds tore through the air as return fire answered back.

Several rounds from the shooters in the Impala hit a man running in the opposite direction. Snead pulled his firearm out of the holster and trained it on the vehicle. Then the shooters in the Impala pointed at him and Holmes.

Simultaneously dropping to his knee while smoothly squeezing the trigger in rapid succession, Snead somehow shot the rifle out of the front passenger's hands. The remaining shooter in the Impala fired at him and Holmes as they dove for cover.

Cinder blocks near Holmes's head exploded as he ducked. But a small fragment of the wall embedded itself into Holmes's neck. Blood spurted from the wound. Holmes placed his hand over the gash with his non-gun hand and fired at the Impala.

Snead continued to fire at the car as well. He finished a magazine, reloaded, and kept shooting while searching for better cover.

The second shooter seemed to have difficulty with his AK-47. By the way he was struggling, Snead thought the shooter might have been hit or the gun had jammed.

Snead used the pause to take a good shot.

As the car sped away, shots from both sides of the street hit both the shooter and the driver. The Impala swerved back and forth on the street. It smashed into a power pole, and the driver went through the windshield. Four people dead in less than thirty seconds.

"Tye, you okay?" Snead yelled. He checked Holmes's wound, but it had already stopped bleeding. They both had a few scratches but were okay.

Holmes shook his head. "God damn. Some shit never changes. Those idiots could've killed us."

Snead slowed his breathing and reminded himself he was retired.

I don't miss this one bit, and I don't have to write the report, lucky me.

The police arrived right away and went to work. Snead was a witness instead of a responding officer this time. It felt weird to him.

The officers on scene were previous trainees of his, and he was happy to see they were handling the investigation properly.

Snead and Holmes were asked to remain for the next two hours, so Snead asked about the Caller again.

Holmes sat down on the curb. "I think one of the guys may have called the boss, *Skipper*. I doubt that will help."

Snead didn't know if it would either. "Well, it's something. You ever going to move out of the area? This stuff gets old out here."

Holmes shook his head. "The streets are part of me, man. But I'm pretty sure my wife will force me to move now. These youngsters are crazy, and I'm too old for it."

The investigating officers told Holmes and Snead they could leave. Snead thanked Holmes and hightailed it back to his house with a new piece of evidence. He'd run with the name "Skipper."

CHAPTER TWENTY-SIX

Hank's Place, a restaurant and bar, was a cozy dive and one of the few options in town. This surprised Dix. Andros was one of the biggest islands in the Bahamas, but one of the least populated. Many small businesses were seasonal.

The guys were enjoying their beer and burgers when Martin barged in. He appeared extremely intoxicated to Dix, gaining speed, but stumbling and falling about three-quarters of the way to the bar. Suzie, who'd followed him in, helped him up and then escorted him to where everyone was seated.

Dix pointed to the stool next to him. "Please, sit down." Suzie helped Martin get seated, then he told Dix, Petersen, and the local officers a little about what Preston's girlfriend had said. "She was completely freaked out... mentioned UAVs and the Coast Guard. The girl had also spent a lot of time with Preston and knew he was running drugs, but didn't care because he provided for her and her baby. She was confident the Caller was connected to the Coast Guard."

Dix nodded. "This evidence, as well as other small pieces of the puzzle, seems to point to the Coast Guard. I guess we should focus on them."

Martin glanced around and looked at Dix. "Listen, man, can I talk to you alone real quick?"

"Sure, what's up?"

They moved to a dark corner away from the bar.

Martin checked around again, then moved close to Dix. "She didn't tell anyone but me. She says the local cops are in on this, and she doesn't trust them."

Dix was skeptical, but it made sense. "That doesn't surprise me. There's a lot of money involved."

Martin was a mess. "I have her contact information, but if you want to talk to her some more, you should let her pick a place and go and see her alone."

"Is there anything else? I should get back to the locals. I won't say anything about what you just told me." Martin handed Dix a piece of paper and called to Suzie to take him home.

Dix rejoined the group. "You guys ever see any drones flying around?"

A couple guys nodded. "Interesting," said Dix.

Before they could continue, the local officers were dispatched to an incident at another bar on the other side of the island. They ran out and sped away with lights flashing and sirens blaring.

CHAPTER TWENTY-SEVEN

Bubba and Wilfred had traveled all over the islands, for business and pleasure, ever since they were kids. They traversed the line between legal and illegal activities on a daily basis, but mostly stayed on the side of the law. Nevertheless, they knew who to ask to learn more about the Caller.

His name was Jay Remy. Remy had been a dealer since he was fifteen. With two prison terms under his belt, he'd vowed to live a life of secrecy after being paroled for the second time.

Bubba knew a few dives where Remy might be found, but the first three they checked revealed nothing. The situation pissed Bubba off.

Meanwhile, Wilfred called everyone he could think of who might know where Remy was hanging out these days.

Bubba patted Wilfred on the shoulder. "Bro, we gotta find Remy so we can get something on this Caller."

Wilfred hung up on another unsuccessful call. "I know. Maybe we'll get lucky, but Remy is lying real low. It's good because that means he's back running dope. I'm sure he knows something."

Bubba didn't respond.   He saw one of his childhood friends walking outside a converted warehouse known for prostitution. The place was used primarily by visitors to the island looking for a little paid fun.

Bubba flagged the guy over. He and Wilfred got out of the car. Counting on drug use in connection with prostitution on Andros, he knew Remy was at the center of both. Bubba asked his friend if he'd seen "Money," Remy's nickname.

"Yeah. Saw him in a pearl white Cadillac Escalade in the alley."

As Bubba was about to ask him other places Remy might be or where he was dealing, Wilfred tapped him on the shoulder and pointed down the street.

Bubba saw the vehicle they'd been talking about cruise slowly about a block away.

His friend followed Bubba's gaze. "There he go right there."

A kid approached the driver's window of the Cadillac, and a drug deal appeared to go down as he and the driver handed something to each other.

Bubba and Wilfred jumped into the car and Bubba put it in gear. He didn't want to be too obvious, so he followed at a distance. As the white vehicle continued, a few more people approached it and appeared to do hand-to-hand deals with the driver.

The Cadillac sped away. Bubba did what he could to stay with it but saw a Royal Bahamian Police Force car pull directly behind it and turn their lights and sirens on.

The SUV pulled over, and the officers exited their police vehicle and approached Remy's Cadillac. Bubba and Wilfred watched as both officers went up to the driver's door.

"What the hell are these guys doing?" asked Wilfred. He knew two-man units would never go up to the same door.

"Don't know," answered Bubba.

Wilfred pointed to a spot at the curb several cars back from their targets. "Let's chill here so we can see what's happening. Something's not right."

Bubba pulled over and stopped.

They watched as Remy handed one of the cops a manila envelope. The men joked for a few minutes, shook hands with the driver, and got back into their patrol car. They drove away, and the Escalade continued north.

Bubba followed for about six miles until the Cadillac abruptly pulled over, and Remy jumped out. He began swaggering back toward Bubba and Wilfred.

His blazer jacket bulged, and he held something in his right hand.

Wilfred grabbed his gun.

Remy yelled, "You boys want to talk?" He motioned for them to meet him outside their vehicle.

Wilfred looked straight at Remy. "He looks pretty pissed."

Bubba turned off the key. "Let's talk. That's what we came for."

Remy put his right hand behind his back. "Bubba, what's got you following me?"

Bubba and Wilfred kept their eyes on Remy's hands. "We need to talk," Bubba replied. "Okay. But in my truck."

Bubba and Wilfred both shook their heads. "No, we do it right here," said Will.

Remy chuckled. "Okay then, but this better be quick. I need to make some more money tonight."

They walked toward him. *This ought to me interesting,* thought Bubba.

CHAPTER TWENTY-EIGHT

Eating dinner with his wife in a romantic setting helped Pierce forget about work.

His cell phone vibrated reminding him he had two agents in a foreign country working a drug case they probably shouldn't be involved with. Pierce told his wife he wanted to take her home. He gave her a little wink, hoping to distract her.

As he drove home, he was making plans, expecting to make love to her. He knew he would be tied up for the next few days and would be in serious trouble if he didn't make her feel special. When he left the room, his wife said, "Go get him, honey. We'll get together again *after* you catch him."

Pierce smiled and gave her a long kiss and hug.

He went to his living room, wanting an update from Dix before figuring out what was needed next. When he called Dix, no one answered.

Pierce had thought about the case at length. He wanted help from Jim Calhoun based on what he understood about the size and sophistication of what Dix and Petersen were dealing with. Pierce dialed Calhoun. The phone rang three times, and a new voicemail message played. "I'm sorry I missed your call. I'm on vacation for two weeks. If this is an emergency, please call my secretary, explain the issue, and she'll relay the message."

Pierce found this very odd. Calhoun never took time off, except once to attend his daughter's funeral. *That must have been about fifteen or twenty years ago.*

On to Plan B. Trouble was, he didn't have a Plan B. He wasn't able to help Dix or Petersen. He felt useless. *Come on, man, get your shit together and make something happen.*

Pierce climbed into his unmarked undercover vehicle and drove toward downtown Miami, hoping to find a local dealer to hit up for information about large local suppliers.

It took him about twenty minutes to find a guy he classified as a mid-level dealer. Pierce had busted him before and this guy liked to talk in an effort to keep from going to jail.

Pierce watched the man from afar and determined he was selling narcotics again. He called dispatch and asked for backup. Then he turned on his dash cam. Once it was obvious the guy was dealing, Pierce decided to take him down.

He surprised the suspect right in the middle of a transaction and was out of the car and had the guy in handcuffs before he had any clue Pierce was there.

As Pierce was about to advise dispatch of his location and status, an unmarked Ford Crown Victoria screeched to a halt behind him. All four doors opened and members of his team sprang out and chased the customer who'd just made the purchase away.

The man immediately pointed to the dealer in the back of Pierce's car. "I just bought from him. He's been selling for years down here."

Pierce looked at the dealer and smiled. "Boys, take that guy to the precinct. I'll take this one in myself."

The dealer looked nervous and was sweating profusely.

This is going to be fun, thought Pierce.

CHAPTER TWENTY-NINE

Snead clicked the Google shortcut on his desktop and waited a few seconds as the browser loaded on his screen. In the search bar, he typed: Coast Guard, U.S. Navy, Skipper and hit enter.

Two hundred sixty-one thousand web pages contained these words popped up. Snead was not happy. He sifted through several of the top sites and learned the term skipper was mostly used when addressing the captain of a ship. It was not commonly used today.

It appeared in Coast Guard jargon because not all cutters had a captain. So the men began calling the person in charge a skipper. It seemed to be another connection to the Coast Guard. Tyrone Holmes had heard it almost fifteen years earlier, so it was even more likely the men who used the term were Coast Guard seamen.

Snead now searched to see who might have been in charge of Coast Guard cutters fifteen years before. He'd then try to eliminate names from the list he got from the MIT guys of who had access to the computer where the online transaction for the registration of the speedboat originated. It was a daunting task. Snead shook his head in disgust.

The only name he didn't have to check was Jim Calhoun.

He'd crossed off the name as soon as he received the faxed list. *There's no way the guy could be involved in this crap.*

One item that popped up was a number to contact the Coast Guard for general questions. After being re-directed for five minutes, he finally spoke to a live person. He asked for a list of previous captains or skippers of cutters. The secretary said she'd never heard the term skipper before and asked what a cutter was.

Snead rolled his eyes, glad that she couldn't see him. "How about this? Are Coast Guard records archived on a database accessible via the internet?"

She paused a second. "I'm afraid I don't know the answer. You see, I've only been here for a few days."

"May I speak to your supervisor?"

The woman paused. "Well, she's not here right now." Snead persisted.

"When will she be back?"

"I don't know. She's been gone awhile. Wait a second. I hear her coming."

Snead perked up. "Excellent. I'd like to talk to her."

"Sure. Please hold."

"How may I help you?" The woman sounded a bit out of breath.

Snead tried to be charming. "My name is Sergeant Andrew Snead from the Miami-Dade Police Department. I'm sorry to bother you. I have a few questions."

"What kind of information are you looking for? Our systems aren't as modernized as some agencies. However, we may be able to help depending on what you need."

Snead hoped this would work. "I'm looking for a list of all captains and skippers of Coast Guard cutters over the past twenty years."

The woman whistled. "If we're talking that far back, there is a record, but it's not automated, at least not yet."

Snead scowled. "Are the records in a vault or in storage?"

"They're in a storage unit in Virginia. The last time I checked, Florida was a long way from Virginia."

Snead chuckled. "Okay, thanks. May I ask another question?"

"Sure, go ahead."

"If I email you a list of names, can you identify the people who are no longer with the Coast Guard?"

"I guess. Can you tell me what this is all about, or is it classified?"

Snead laughed out loud. "If I told you, I'd have to kill you."

She laughed. "You'd better bring an army. I like guns and know how to use them."

Snead wrote down her email address. She said she could get to the list after lunch. That gave him time to surf the internet some more and get a bite to eat.

CHAPTER THIRTY

Jorge Blanco, John Lester, Tim Simpson, Paul Kemp, and David Timms studied an ops plan from a top-level clearance mission recently assigned to their unit. They'd been hand-picked by Rear Admiral Tony Charles and led by Blanco.

As missions went, this appeared to be fairly mundane. They had to infiltrate a storage unit currently being guarded by the Royal Bahamian Police Force. Several informants used by the Coast Guard revealed a handful of local officers were helping someone plan to steal the narcotics inside. Blanco's team would safeguard the cocaine. But they could not advise the local police commissioner for fear the mission would be compromised. Once secured, the narcotics would stay on a cutter, heavily guarded, until the investigation was concluded. The cutter would remain off the coast of Andros Island. *I wonder why they just don't ask the locals to hold the drugs in a safer location*, thought Blanco.

The area containing the cocaine was bugged and surrounded by cameras, but the locals would present the biggest challenge. Blanco figured they could easily disable the surveillance equipment and take out a few corrupt cops. The problem was they had to do it all and not be detected.

They could not be caught or identified. If it happened, they'd be left to fend for themselves, and all record of their association with the Coast Guard or the United States military would be eliminated. This elite team was told any equipment available to the Coast Guard and U.S. Navy would be available to them. The ultimate objective was to seize the cocaine, which would be used later in an independent investigation by DEA, CIA, and Coast Guard.

Jorge Blanco had the most experience and was, therefore, the leader of the unit. The other men had worked with him in Afghanistan and Syria. They had experimental training on a regular basis, taking them to all corners of the earth.

Blanco stood. "You shitheads think you can pull this off without screwing it up?"

Simpson muttered, "Get bent. If anyone's going to jack this up, it'd be you."

The other men laughed. Then Kemp asked, "You think this is a setup?"

Blanco answered, "Relax. I'm sure this is another training mission. The serious shit you signed up for will come soon enough."

Timms asked, "When are we supposed to start the festivities?"

Blanco glanced at his watch. "We leave at zero six hundred in three days. We're on standby status until then, meaning the big bosses could send us earlier. Keep your cell phones on and handy so I can update you if needed. When I get the call, I'll contact you."

One by one the men got up from their seats, grabbed their duffel bags and other gear, and left the briefing room. Blanco stayed behind to develop a game plan and contact Jim Calhoun. *Sooner or later they're going to have to give us a real mission. These training ones are getting old.*

CHAPTER THIRTY-ONE

As Dix and Petersen left the bar, they spotted Roger's car and waved him over.

"Give us a lift?" Dix asked. "Sure. Hop in."

Roger looked them over. "You guys look beat. When did you sleep last?"

Petersen settled into the back seat and laid his head against it. "Feels like at least a year." He closed his eyes.

Roger started the car. "While you've been drinking at the local hot spot, I went by the storage facility. DEA agents working with the locals outfitted the place with surveillance equipment. When I told the DEA boys I'd see you, they said to tell you there's a small container close to my house. It's filled with all the equipment you might need. And I have your firearms and body armor."

Dix frowned. "Why would DEA agents give all this information to you?"

Roger squirmed. "Well, there's more to all of this, but I can't let you in on it until the timing's right."

Dix all but shouted. "Fuck this. When I wake up tomorrow, my bags are packed, and you guys can deal with this mess. We gave up our vacation to help out. Shit, we've done most of this stuff on our own despite the local authorities. As far as I'm concerned, you can stop the damn car right here, and I'll walk back to the lodge."

Petersen roused. "I'm with Dix. We're not the bad guys here, and we need answers."

Roger looked nervous but apologetic. "Look, I know it wasn't right. The DEA agents have used you two but kept what they knew hidden. I'll tell you everything."

"What do you mean used us? What do you have?" Dix asked.

"Five or six local officers have been dealing or stealing drugs. DEA and the local higher-ups asked me to help identify them. That's why I know a few of their people."

Dix frowned again. "You could have told us. The secrets on this island are pissing me off."

Roger shook his head. "No. I was ordered not to."

"Anything else?"

Roger nodded. "Yes. My DEA contacts have been monitoring a Coast Guard rear admiral named Charles for about a year. He seems to be connected to the bad cops in some way. A few DEA agents vacationed in the Bahamas and set up surveillance on Andros, Exuma, and a few other islands. When the speedboat was stored yesterday, a .50 caliber 12.7 mm BMG round was found splintered near the engine block. According to DEA, the Coast Guard is the largest user of the rifle that shoots those. They also figure it would take a special unit to hijack the speedboat. The rear admiral, this Charles guy, is in charge of those units. DEA calls them rogue units."

Dix considered what Roger had told him and the clues they'd been collecting. He was already pretty sure the Caller had ties to the Coast Guard; this almost sealed it for him.

They pulled up to the lodge. Dix knew he had to get sleep before his system completely crashed.

The detectives slowly stumbled out of the car. Dix patted Roger on the shoulder, and they headed to their cottage. Dix looked back over his shoulder. "Wake us if anything significant develops. Petersen and I are going to hit the hay for a few hours. And no more secrets, please."

CHAPTER THIRTY-TWO

As the G5 jet reached cruising altitude, Calhoun began getting updates from his sources in the Coast Guard, Royal Navy, and the Royal Bahamian Police Force.

His secure line rang. "Go ahead."

He recognized Jorge Blanco's voice. "Sir, the unit is briefed and has developed an operational model. We're packed and racked for deployment. Still awaiting word from Charles to deploy."

"Very good. I'm not entirely sure if you boys will see action, but I'm glad to know you're ready. This mission is intended for stealth, and not firepower and fireworks."

"Understood. The men are on standby when needed."

"Fantastic. I'll notify Charles." He hung up.

The phone rang again. "Go ahead."

An adult male voice spoke. "We've got an issue, sir. Footage from the UAV of raising the speedboat showed two unknown white male adults in the mix. We checked and found out these guys are narcotics detectives from Miami-Dade. One is a newbie, Steve Petersen. The other is Bill Dix."

"The same Bill Dix from Miami-Dade PD who's been in the paper?" Calhoun had read about a couple of his cases.

"Affirmative."

"Okay, what else do you know?"

"It seems everyone from DEA to the locals on Andros is hunting a guy named the Caller. They think he's a major drug distributor."

Calhoun raised an eyebrow. "Anything else?"

"Unfortunately, yes. Two Royal Bahamian Police Force officers we've used in the past have gone missing. We heard rumors they were picked up by DEA."

God damn it. Could anything else go wrong?

"Oh, and investigators retrieved a splintered 12.7 mm round from the speedboat. They've already assumed it was a Coast Guard issue."

Calhoun shook his head. "The next time I ask for an update, just tell me to remember what happened this time."

The man on the other end chuckled. Then he suddenly became quiet. Calhoun noticed the stillness. "What's up?"

No answer.

Calhoun reacted quickly. "Get rid of the cell phone and leave your location *now*."

Across the line, he heard loud knocking followed by, "Search warrant. This is the police. Open up."

Calhoun had hung up before he heard the outcome. His contact was a mid-level drug dealer and pimp who had DEA and Coast Guard connections because two of his sisters had married men in those agencies. This guy had met Calhoun, and it was probably only a matter of time before he'd cave to interrogation. But, Calhoun wasn't sure they could get the information and process it before he retrieved the cocaine from the speedboat. The operation would take two days, and Calhoun hoped the authorities wouldn't be able to find a link to him by then. He determined the man would give them false information to cover Calhoun's tracks.

However, he moved up the plans to attack the storage unit to the following day just to be sure. He filled his son in on the changes over his Bluetooth as Junior piloted the G5 jet to Andros.

Calhoun finished with, "You see any problems stepping up the retrieval to tomorrow night instead of the next day?"

His son shook his head. "No."

"Son, I've thought about our last conversation. I'm considering retiring and letting you keep the business." It was a lie, but he wanted the kid focused on the current operation.

"I'm glad. I won't let you down. Fasten your seat belt. We're on final approach to Mangrove Cay. According to the contacts on the island, there are lots of local cops in the area. More than usual, and even some added surveillance equipment, too."

Calhoun checked his seat belt and prepared for landing. The changes seemed normal based on what should be done when an agency finds an enormous stash of cocaine. "Continue as planned, son."

The plane landed smoothly and taxied to the end of the runway. When the door opened, Calhoun and his pilot were met by eight Royal Bahamian officers. Calhoun noticed the fully armed men appeared unfriendly. *Play it cool*.

CHAPTER THIRTY-THREE

Pierce questioned his arrestee on the way to the precinct. The guy was looking at a minimum of three felonies based on Pierce's observations. He'd consider lessening some of the charges if the guy talked, and he had hoped the man's information would be useful for the case in the Bahamas.

Before they reached the precinct, Pierce pulled over and turned to face the guy in the back seat. "Listen, Chad, you and I have been playing the same game for ten years. Sometimes I cut you a break, but tonight I'm gonna put you away for the rest of your life."

Chad was breathing heavily. "Okay, okay. No bullshit. What's it going to take for some of this stuff to go bye-bye?"

"You can start by telling me who the big guy is."

Chad shook his head. "Come on, man. I'm dead if I say anything."

Pierce smirked. "You already have by telling me the supplier is male. Cut the crap, Chad, or I'll see to it you qualify for a life sentence."

Chad was squirmy and nervous. "Dude, calm down. All right. Listen, why the questions about the supplier? You usually target dealers."

Pierce snapped back. "I'm asking the questions, pal. You've got until we reach the station to tell me something useful. Otherwise, no deals." He started the car and pulled out onto the street.

Chad hesitated. "Look. There's one guy who only deals cocaine. He's been in the business as long as you've been a cop. I met him for a big transaction. I had a chunk of cash, thirty large, and he had kilos for sale."

"When did you meet this guy? And what do you remember about it?"

"About ten years ago. Remember when you caught me the first time? I bought the stuff from him."

"What do you remember about the guy?"

Chad seemed to gain momentum. "There were three guys. Two just watched the main guy's back. They looked like badasses, buff with short haircuts. They had some serious weapons too, MP-5s, I think. I showed them the money, and the big man showed me the coke. He sold me a full brick for only thirty thousand."

Pierce was skeptical. "Why do you remember all that? It was ten years ago, and you've sniffed a lot of junk since then." He watched Chad stiffen in his mirror.

"It was something about the cocaine, the way it was packaged. It had a red horse head on it, pressed into the center of the brick when I opened it. Over the years, I saw lots more like it. This guy's been pumping coke into Miami for as long as I can remember."

Pierce now had a lead with the red horse head. "Did they speak during the transaction?"

"Yeah, but very little."

"Do you remember any of the conversation?"

Chad noticed they'd arrived at the precinct. "If I remember right, the main guy's cell phone, an old brick type, rang constantly. When the deal went down, one of the muscle men answered and said, 'Go ahead. You've reached the Caller.'"

Pierce slammed on the brakes and spun around to face his prisoner. "What did you just say?"

"The guy said, 'Go ahead. You've reached the Caller.'"

Pierce tried not to show his excitement. "If you saw a picture of these guys, would you be able to point them out?" Chad shook his head. "I don't know for sure. I think I saw the big guy again about six years later, but I don't remember where."

Pierce took Chad inside and questioned him for another thirty minutes. He booked the twists of cocaine he'd found on Chad as property slated for destruction. Pierce considered putting together a lineup, but Chad was too high to keep his eyes open long enough to stare at the random photos. Plus,

Pierce didn't have any idea who the suspect was to prepare a proper lineup anyway.
    He decided to call Dix to give him an update.

CHAPTER THIRTY-FOUR

Remy moved closer to his truck and tried to keep a safe distance from Bubba and Wilfred. He tossed around the idea of killing the two guys and making a run for it. They meant nothing to him and were expendable. But he owed Bubba for testifying in his defense a few years earlier. Plus, he didn't want to clean their blood off his custom leather seats. So he decided against it... for now.

When Bubba started asking him about the Caller, Remy was more than happy to tell them everything he knew about the cheating, lying bastard. Remy wanted vengeance. "He's a real prick. Last year, we did an arranged drop. I gave him a hundred grand cash, and he gave me the worst coke I've ever seen. I barely made my money back."

Wilfred nodded. "You've been lookin' for him ever since." Remy smiled. "Of course. I want his head on a platter.

Everyone I talk to has no idea who he really is or where he's based. All I know is he doesn't live on the islands."

Remy glanced toward Bubba and noticed the big man eyeing him closely.

Wilfred interrupted. "We're pretty sure the Caller hired a sniper to hijack the go-fast Sean and

Preston were on. The sniper screwed up, killed both of them and sank the boat."

Remy interrupted. "The one stored downtown?" Wilfred nodded again. "Yep. It's there to lure the Caller."

Remy laughed. "So why all the questions about who he is? If he shows up to get the dope, it won't matter because you'll know."

Wilfred took a step in his direction. "The problem is he may work for the Coast Guard. We'd have a much better chance of actually catching him if we knew who we were looking for."

Remy smirked. "It won't matter when he's caught. That is, if he comes."

Bubba spoke at last. "Dey not sure he'll come. Dey think he might send someone else."

Remy frowned. "So if the trap doesn't work, they'll still need an actual person to hunt down."

Wilfred stepped back next to Bubba and nodded. "Exactly. You know anything that might link your guy to the Coast Guard?"

Remy stared at Bubba but answered Wilfred. "You could be right. With all the deals he's done in the Bahamas, it seems strange he's never been caught. He's been going for at least ten years without any problems. The only explanation of how only his drugs get through is if he has connections with the bastards patrolling the water."

Wilfred cleared his throat. "Well, thanks for your time. I bet you have business to attend to. You know where to reach us if you think of anything else."

Remy got back into his truck while eyeing Bubba.

Wilfred called out. "Thanks. We won't forget your help when it all comes down."

"Just stay away from my business." Remy roared off.

CHAPTER THIRTY-FIVE

Dix woke up first. From the position of the sun and the sounds of the birds chirping wildly, he figured it was close to seven o'clock. He thought about waking Petersen, but he didn't need him right now. He showered, dressed, and walked over to the main house to see if he could scrounge up something to eat.

Several other guests were already awake. He passed one guy tying a Tarpon pattern on an Abel vise. Another stood on the deck overlooking Elliott Creek practicing his casting. Dix followed the scent of freshly brewed coffee. A counter in the lobby held the urn and cups as well as warm homemade cinnamon rolls. He'd scarfed down two cups of coffee and a couple of rolls before Petersen joined him. Dix wiped his mouth. "How'd you sleep?"

"Like shit. I kept having odd dreams about my ex."

To lighten the mood, Dix replied, "Well, if it helps any, I was thinking about her too." He chuckled.

Petersen gave him the bird. "You don't ever let up, do you? Anyway, let's get back to this Caller guy."

"I've got a feeling we're going to catch some major flak for taking this guy down. The list of people he's controlling seems to get longer as we dig. There may be some political figures, both here and in the United States, whose heads will roll before it's over."

Petersen nodded as he took a bite out of his own roll. "Too many people have died and are still dying because of this guy. His greed will do him in. He has to be unbelievably wealthy after all his years of trafficking. But he won't let this load go."

Dix nodded, then stood to get himself one more cup. After all, who knew when they'd stop long enough to eat again?

When he returned, Petersen said, "I'll call Roger, Bubba, and Wilfred. You call our boss and Snead."

Dix grimaced. "I'll make the calls. Pierce won't be happy." Petersen shrugged. "Oh well, get it done."

Dix raised an eyebrow. "Yes, sir."

Petersen laughed. "I must admit I enjoy watching you two butt heads."

Dix laughed. "Piss off." He left and went outside to make his calls.

The first person he reached was Sergeant Pierce.

"Hey Dix, how the hell are you? I snagged a mid-level guy dealing in Liberty City last night. He had some information you might find interesting about your guy."

Dix noticed Pierce was being unusually pleasant and wondered why. "What did he tell you?"

Pierce filled him in on the details.

Dix whistled. "Someone else called him the Caller on his own without prompting?"

"Right."

Dix was impressed. "Good. It looks like you've made the Miami connection."

"My guy bought a kilo from your guy. Stamped into it was a red horse head."

Now Dix was totally intrigued. "We found the same horse head on the coke we recovered from the speedboat."

"This guy, Chad, saw the group of guys pretty well, but it was a long time ago. He said even though it's been ten years, he thinks he could identify him if he saw him again, say in a lineup."

"Wow. Do you really think he could ID the guy?" *Ten years is a long time.*

"He's used and sold cocaine for a long time. I think if you get the Caller, my guy pointing him out will help get a conviction. Or at least connect some dots."

Dix was genuinely appreciative. "Thanks, Sarge. I'll let you know what I have here after I talk to everyone else. Keep your guy handy, okay?"

Pierce growled. "I told Chad not to leave the city. Otherwise, I'd have an arrest warrant issued." Pierce hung up before Dix could comment.

Dix smiled. There's the boss man I know and love.

CHAPTER THIRTY-SIX

Snead had been trying to track down the mastermind through the internet with little success. He contemplated what to do next. Then his phone rang.

"Dix here. What have you got?"

"Nothing. What's going on in the Bahamas?"

"All kinds of stuff. You doing all right? You sound sort of down."

"I'm fine. Just hit a bump in the road and was getting pissy."

Dix said, "I talked to Michael Pierce. He's been working the streets in Miami and found a dealer who made a connection to the guy were looking for. Apparently the dealer Pierce arrested did a transaction with our guy about ten years ago. He bought a kilo. It had a red horse head on it."

"Didn't you guys find something like that on the cocaine from the speedboat?" Snead asked.

"Yep. Pierce's dealer also said while they were in the middle of the transaction, the guy he was buying the dope from got a call on his cell phone. One of the other guys answered and said something like, 'Go ahead. You've reached the Caller.'"

"Interesting. Did he think the guys might be military?"

"Yes." Dix nodded his head.

"So another connection to the military, dope with the same stamp as the stuff on the boat in the Bahamas, and the actual mention of someone as the Caller. That's a shitload of circumstantial evidence, but hard to prove in court."

Dix hesitated. "Your guy said he thought he could identify who we think may have been the Caller. If we make a bust and do a lineup, we might get lucky."

Snead snorted. "Now that would be good for the jury trial."

Dix continued. "Other than that, I don't have much. I asked Petersen to continue checking what happened locally while we got some shuteye."

Snead realized it was his turn to share additional discoveries with Dix. "I was poking around in Liberty City and ran into Tyrone Holmes. You remember the guy. He told me he did a deal with a guy about fifteen years ago. Sounds similar to what Pierce's guy said. There was one guy in charge, and two guys that watched his back. Tye said they were muscular and had military haircuts."

"Really? Sounds like too many similarities to be a coincidence."

"Damned right. Tye also said one of the bodyguards called the boss 'Skipper.' I did a little investigating and found out the term was commonly used by Coast Guard seamen when referring to the person in charge of a cutter. Sometimes somebody other than a captain was in charge, so the crewmen called the person Skipper. Anyway, it's another possible Coast Guard connection."

"Hmm. I keep coming back to the same conclusion. I'm afraid our bad guy is going to turn out to be thought of as a good guy in most circles. Whoever it is has too much knowledge of what all of us do."

Snead had hoped the perpetrator wasn't in law enforcement or the military. "I contacted the main Coast Guard center to get confirmation about the use of the word *Skipper*. I also received a list of names from my computer-savvy friends of people who had access to the computer used to register the speedboat."

"How come you always have a connection? Never mind. I don't want to know. Any names of interest?"

Snead chuckled, then grew serious. "The 'Bloodhound,' but I crossed him off immediately. There's no way he'd be stupid enough to get involved in something like this. He literally *is* the Coast Guard."

"Wasn't the name used for the registration Jackie Spears, Jim Calhoun's daughter?" Dix asked.

"Yeah, but all the names used were of deceased people, so this could have been random."

"Okay, what else do you know?"

"I sent the list to a Coast Guard secretary. She just emailed it back while we've been talking." Snead paused to open the file attachment to his email. "Most of the names are marked off, meaning they no longer work for the Coast Guard, so they don't fit our profile. Four names are left. The only one of real interest is Rear Admiral Tony Charles. I heard he's running a new unit. It's supposed to be like the SEALS, but for the Coast Guard."

"Do you remember the guy, Roger, who caught the sniper?"

"Yeah, why?"

"Turns out he's retired law enforcement and Royal Navy.

Now he's a consultant for the DEA. His people have been investigating some local police officers and some Coast Guard people. One of the names he mentioned was Tony Charles."

Snead slapped his knee. "The finger seems to point at Charles. Does anyone know where he is right now? Someone should keep an eye on him, and maybe even let him figure out he's being watched."

"I'll mention it."

Snead still planned to check the other names. "Just to cover our butts, I'll look into the other guys on this list. If I learn anything, I'll call you back."

"Okay, thanks for your help."

* * * *

Dix hung up and went to see what Petersen was up to. He walked down the dock and heard Petersen's voice.

Based on his end of the conversation, it sounded like he was talking to Wilfred or Bubba. As he rounded the corner, he saw Petersen on his cell phone. He didn't want to interrupt, so he picked up a fly rod and began casting in Elliott Creek while he worked on the case in his head. He managed to hook a bonefish, and it took off up the creek before snapping his line. For a moment, he felt like he was on vacation again.

Petersen finished his call and walked over to Dix. "We gotta talk."

So much for the vacation.

"I spoke to Wilfred and Bubba. They said they ran into one of the biggest dealers on Andros, and he provided some information."

Dix raised an eyebrow and began chewing his nails. "Those guys seem overly resourceful. I wonder what they do when no one is watching."

Petersen shrugged and continued. "Apparently the guy we're looking for has been working in the Caribbean for over ten years, maybe longer. Their contact said he primarily uses boats to move narcotics."

"Did the dealer say anything we don't already know?" "He told Bubba and Wilfred the boats carrying the Caller's narcotics are never stopped. The guy said there was no way he could get all his dope through without actually being involved with one of the agencies patrolling the water and knowing their schedules and tactics. The dealer said he did some checking on the guy."

"Let me guess, the Caller did him dirty."

Petersen grinned and nodded. "Yup, and the dealer said the Caller probably had access to the UAVs being used by the Coast Guard or made the decisions on where the Coast Guard boats would patrol. He said *everyone* gets caught sometimes, but not the Caller."

Dix wasn't impressed. "Well, it's just theory from a drug dealer. If it's spot on, then it's another connection to the Coast Guard. I'm thinking we need to focus on Coast Guard people. For all we know, the Caller may already be in the area watching everything unfold."

Petersen continued with his update. "I also called Roger. He said they, meaning the DEA, picked up the two local officers they'd been watching late last night. Roger said they questioned them at length. They admitted working for the Caller, and gave up the name of a mid-level dealer in Liberty City, who corroborated the information."

Dix straightened up. "That's great work."

Petersen replied, "Whatever they said must have been verifiable because they got a search warrant for the dealer's place in Miami. It was served early this morning. They kicked in the door and found the guy on the phone with someone, who they now think was the Caller."

"Why do they think that?"

"Apparently, they detained the guy and grabbed his cell phone before he could destroy it. The preliminary information is the line was secured using technology only available to a small, elite group, primarily head honchos in places like the CIA, DEA, Special OPS, SEALS, and of course, the Coast Guard. It's experimental and extremely hard to trace, which is why they suspect these guys were using it in the first place. They told Roger it might be a few days before their specialists figure it out. It's time we don't have."

Dix worried that time was about up on this charade. "Did they jam the guy to see what he knows about our Caller?"

"Yes, but he lawyered up right away. He knows who we're looking for, which makes him valuable, but he's not talking, at least not right now."

"He'll eventually turn over and become the star witness for the prosecution, probably for full immunity," said Dix.

Petersen continued, "With what's on the table and the charges he's looking at, I'm pretty sure his lawyer will tell him to take a deal. The only problem is, it will all be done down the road, which doesn't help us right now."

Dix made up his mind. "We should focus on Coast Guard people, particularly this Charles guy."

Petersen nodded. "I agree. We need to check all the Coast Guard personnel on the island. We should also double check the storage facility."

Dix agreed, so they called Roger to take them on another ride.

The old car he'd loaned them wouldn't start.

When he showed up, he told Dix and Petersen things were moving quickly. "The attorney for the guy apprehended in Miami reached out to the Feds and wants to negotiate a plea deal." *Wow, that was quick. Maybe too quick.*

CHAPTER THIRTY-SEVEN

Jim Calhoun never got too excited about anything. He and his son saw the officers and weren't concerned. They met the men with smiles.

Calhoun stepped off the plane. "Good evening, gentlemen. I'm Jim Calhoun, Lieutenant Commander of the Coast Guard. Anyone know where your boss is so I can get up to speed on the operation?"

A few of the local officers had no idea who Calhoun was and asked him for identification.

Before he made a move to retrieve it, another officer shook his head and waved him on. He told the others they were talking to a legend, Jim 'Bloodhound' Calhoun. When the others heard the name 'Bloodhound,' they looked embarrassed.

Calhoun thought the exchange was funny. *This is going to be much easier than I thought.*

An officer got on the radio and asked for a supervisor to respond to the airport immediately. When he finished, he told the other officers to extend professional courtesy to their guest.

Calhoun shook hands with the policemen while his son loaded their equipment into a black Yukon Denali parked next to their jet. The cops didn't know it, but the Denali was custom-made, with bullet-resistant windows, run-flat tires, and reinforced doors.

The vehicle was a luxurious tank and had been parked there the evening before by one of the people on Calhoun's payroll after being flown in from Miami.

Twenty minutes passed, and Calhoun spotted a car barreling toward the airport.

Calhoun and his son noticed the signage on the side door as it pulled up. The local police commissioner had arrived.

A very large Bahamian man exited the right rear door. Of all the people Calhoun had seen so far with badges, this was the first who looked professional.

The large gentleman extended his hand. "Mr. Calhoun, I'm Commissioner Knowles. It's my great pleasure to meet you. Welcome to the Bahamas. We've confiscated some cocaine and hope you will help us spring a trap on the people we expect to arrive to retrieve it."

Calhoun wanted to explore just how much these people knew about his operation. He shook the commissioner's hand firmly. *These poor people have no idea.*

"Do we have any information about the suspect?"

"Not really. There's been significant speculation, but we don't have much."

Calhoun shook his head. "So we're looking for a person without a lead and have no idea if or when he will try to take the cocaine you have in custody?"

The commissioner looked down. "I'm afraid so. We have the assistance of two detectives from Florida, who think the guy people here refer to as the Caller, might actually be employed by your agency."

Calhoun raised his eyebrow and feigned shock. "With the Coast Guard? Where would that come from? It takes a set of brass balls to speculate like that."

"To be honest, the two detectives I mentioned have been squeezing information from people here and others working with them have done the same in Miami. They are getting our people up to speed with the updates."

Calhoun needed to meet the detectives. "Are they here now? I'd like to meet them as soon as possible. They work in Miami?"

"They're staying at a local fishing lodge and are eager to meet you as well. With regard to Florida, I've been told Miami-Dade officers have interviewed people and might have some leads. They relayed information to their guys here, and it was told to me."

Calhoun digested the new information. Even if the cops in Florida found and interviewed people who continually purchased from him, the connections would be slight. All leads were to Charles, not him.

By the time anyone figured out he was involved, he'd be gone. Tomorrow he and his son would have the cocaine and be on their way. *It was almost too easy.*

Commissioner Knowles called someone to locate Dix and Petersen. He told Calhoun the two detectives were on their way to the facility where the cocaine was being stored.

Calhoun went with the commissioner while his son stayed behind to make some calls and load the Denali.

✴ ✴ ✴ ✴

Rear Admiral Tony Charles received the call telling him Jim Calhoun made it to Andros Island without a hitch.

Charles called Jorge Blanco. "Jorge, you know where the other men are?"

"Eating dinner, and then they wanted to check out some chicks at the strip club."

Charles was perturbed. "Just what we need, hungry, horny killers. Get them the hell out of there."

"Yes, sir. Consider it done." Blanco cursed the men for taking off to the club.

"Good. Remind them that they're supposed to stay low and operate undetected. Also, Calhoun is going with you guys and is running his own operation. You and your team are in a support role."

"Got it. I'll go gather them. Whatever you need, we're ready and able."

"Excellent. Don't fuck it up."

Blanco shook his head. "Yes, sir."

CHAPTER THIRTY-EIGHT

Andrew Snead had never cared much for Michael Pierce. He thought Pierce rose to sergeant so quickly because he kissed a lot of ass and rode his father's coattails. His old man had been a well-known and respected captain for Miami-Dade PD. Nevertheless, they were working the same case and needed to pool resources.

Snead dialed Pierce's number and half hoped he wouldn't answer.

Pierce answered on the first ring. "Sergeant Pierce. How can I help you?"

"This is Andrew Snead. How are you?"

"Pretty busy, Mr. Snead. What can I do for you?"

"I hoped to meet you to see if we could combine forces to help Dix and Petersen in the Bahamas."

"I understand you've been in communication with my detectives. Dix told me what you'd discovered."

"He told me what you and the team have come up with as well."

"You want to meet at the Donut House in about thirty minutes?"

"I'll be there. Thanks." Pierce hung up.

* * * *

Snead sat at a booth eating a bear claw when he looked up to see Pierce enter. He wiped his face and hands and shook Pierce's hand.

"Can I buy you a cup of Joe to go with that?" Pierce pointed to the pastry.

"No, thanks. The doctor's been trying to wean me off the stuff. He says it's messing up my stomach lining."

Pierce went to the counter and ordered an apple fritter and a large cup of coffee, black. He slid into the booth across from Snead. They started from the beginning and pooled their information.

While wiping a spill with his napkin, Pierce said, "I'd say we're looking for a high-ranking officer in the Coast Guard. The DEA and CIA found a mid-level dealer who's been working with our bad guy for years."

Snead leaned forward. "Is the guy talking?"

"No, he lawyered up. But the DA's office has a monster case against him. They've been asked to strike a deal if he's willing to identify this Caller guy."

Snead whispered, "You heard about the possible connection to Rear Admiral Tony Charles, right?"

Pierce shook his head. "Not much. You got something more to share?"

Snead nodded. "He's on the list I got from the Coast Guard of longtime, high-ranking personnel. The guy's also in charge of the DOG Unit for the Coast Guard."

"DOG Unit?" Pierce drained his cup.

"It's a new unit with the best guys in the Coast Guard designed to compete with SEAL teams. They're supposed to work covertly."

"Interesting."

"My research indicates Charles is the most computer savvy guy in the service, according to some of my MIT sources. The searches I tried for this Caller guy were protected by someone with advanced understanding of computers, networks, and the internet."

Pierce needed more. "So you think it's another connection between Charles and the guy Petersen and Dix think is coming for the dope?"

"Yes." Snead glanced at Pierce's cup. "You want a refill?"

"No, I'm good. I feel more awake now, but the apple fritter landed like a brick."

"I did a little more digging into Charles and learned he has an expensive home and a few toys, like a cigarette boat and two exotic cars. It seems odd he could afford such extravagances on what he makes from the Coast Guard."

Pierce replied, "Maybe it was an inheritance."

"Maybe. I spent a little time in Liberty City last night and ran into Tyrone Holmes."

Pierce looked shocked. "Man, is that guy still alive? I thought he'd have died or been killed by now. He was deep into the drugs fifteen, maybe sixteen years ago."

Snead smiled. "He's alive and hasn't sold dope or used for seven years. He's got a family and a good job. His ear is still to the streets, though. He lives right in the middle of the war zone. From time to time, he gives me information in a roundabout way."

Pierce looked confused. "Did you learn anything about our guy from him?"

"Nothing I can confirm, but he described a drug purchase he made over a decade ago. The guy may have been the drug supplier we're looking for. Tye said he had two bodyguards, and all three of them looked muscular and had short hair. He also said one of the guys called his boss 'Skipper.' Turns out the term was in common use in the Coast Guard at the time Tye bought dope from the guy who could be the Caller."

Pierce rubbed his eyes. "Everything I've heard points toward the Coast Guard. I didn't want to believe someone in the military, especially someone of high rank, would be involved in smuggling drugs but it all points that direction."

Snead twisted his napkin. "I know. It took me a while to wrap my brain around it, but my gut points to the connection. We need to watch Charles closely."

"I hate to agree, but I'm afraid you're right. We need to find where he is. With all the Coast Guard cutters in the Bahamas, I'd guess he's on one of them."

Snead leaned forward. "If Charles is in Florida, would you run surveillance on him?"

Pierce nodded. "I suppose we could do that. My guys could use the practice. The Chief told us to use whatever resources and time we need to assist in this investigation. Apparently the DEA, CIA, Coast Guard, Royal Bahamian Police Force, U.S. Navy, and possibly the FBI are involved in this one. If my guys find him, they'll make the entire department look good."

Snead stood up to leave and offered his hand to Pierce. "I'm going to look into a few other things. If I learn something worthwhile, I'll let you know." The two shook hands.

Pierce got up and said, "And I'll do the same." Snead left the donut shop hoping to stir up more leads for the detectives in the Bahamas.

CHAPTER THIRTY-NINE

Dix watched as an official police vehicle stopped near where he was standing with Petersen. A large, well-built black man and a muscular white man exited.

A beat-up minivan pulled in behind them. Six local officers got out and took defensive positions covering the two occupants of the official police vehicle. The guy Dix recognized as Jim Calhoun wore fatigues. *The man came ready to get dirty.*

Dix, Petersen, and Roger waited while the cadre walked toward them.

Roger whispered to Dix, "The black guy is Commissioner Knowles. I assume the white guy is Jim 'Bloodhound' Calhoun. According to the commissioner, Calhoun is eager to meet you two."

Dix turned. "Petersen, did you hear that? The legendary drug expert wants to meet you."

Petersen grimaced. "Jealousy doesn't suit you, Dix. I hope you'll be on your best behavior."

Dix couldn't reply because Jim Calhoun stood before him with his hand outstretched.

"How the hell are you, Bill?" He looked at Petersen.

"And you must be Detective Petersen."

Dix smiled and shook the proffered hand. "Jim, it's been a long time. I'm doing great. Better now that you're here."

Petersen shook hands with Calhoun, then with Commissioner Knowles. He was surprised. Dix had never mentioned anything about knowing Jim Calhoun.

Calhoun looked at the storage unit. "Is this where the stuff is located? What do we know about it?"

Petersen nodded. "It's over near the speedboat. The boat doesn't function anymore, thanks to a couple careless rounds from a sniper."

Calhoun looked puzzled. "A sniper?"

Dix nodded. "Yeah. A Special Ops sniper named M. A. Thomas." He pointed at Roger. "Roger killed him when the guy had his weapon trained on Petersen and me. We weren't aware of it at the time. If it hadn't been for Roger, we'd probably be dead."

Dix had intentionally left out the part about the interrogation. Calhoun frowned. "So now we have over a thousand kilos of cocaine stored here. You assume this Caller guy will show up looking for it because it's worth at least a hundred million, as I understand it. Anyone know why they call him that?"

Roger shook his head. "Not really. But his only contact seems to be by phone."

Calhoun looked at Dix. "I understand the cargo has been safeguarded by surveillance and audio feeds. I don't see anything visible, which is good. Is there an APS involved?"

The commissioner, Roger, and Petersen looked confused, so Dix said, "He's talking about an alternate power supply." Roger motioned the men to follow him. "I'll point out the system upgrades, straight from the DEA gurus."

Calhoun interrupted. "Just tell me where everything is without pointing it out. If this guy is as advanced as you guys think, he could be watching right now. I'd feel pretty stupid if we made it easy for him. He doesn't need any help from us."

Roger told Calhoun and the commissioner where everything was located and mentioned the backup power supply.

Calhoun turned to the group. "What's the game plan?" Dix answered, "We figure he's coming after dark, possibly by helicopter. He'll probably only take the cocaine. A chopper could land somewhere around the yard, and he will probably attempt to take out the guards, grab the dope and be gone within minutes. The stuff has to be in his possession to convict him of anything but audio and video feeds will gather information to identify this Caller guy. Our navy has several jets ready to scramble to force a plane or helicopter down. If he leaves by boat, you'll handle that."

Calhoun nodded his agreement. "Have you guys seen the schematics for the storage unit and the city streets around it?"

One of the local officers produced them.

Calhoun glanced at the drawings and rubbed his belly. "I'm hungry. Is there someplace we could eat and discuss this some more? I'm buying."

The commissioner suggested a local restaurant, and they all headed there.

As the cars passed the airport, Dix, Roger, and Petersen talked about fly fishing. Petersen mentioned the huge bonefish he let get away. Roger stopped laughing and pointed out the window.

Dix turned to see what he had motioned to. "What's up Roger?"

"Is there a small red horse on the tail of that private jet?"

Petersen's eyes widened. "I'll be damned. That's the horse head we saw on the cocaine." He turned to Roger. "When did that thing get here, and whose is it?"

Dix noticed a U.S. flag next to the red horse head. On the side of the plane were the words, "United States Coast Guard—U.S. Department of

Homeland Security. "Let me guess. Calhoun arrived in that jet."

Roger called Commissioner Knowles. When he hung up, he turned to the detectives. "The commissioner confirmed Mr. Calhoun arrived on it, just him and a pilot. Apparently no one has seen the pilot since it landed."

Dix frowned. "We'll certainly have something to talk about at lunch, won't we?"

Petersen looked at his partner. "Just how do you intend to question a living legend about arriving in an expensive plane with the same horse head on it as on the cocaine?"

Dix got a broad smile. "Watch and learn, my friend.

Watch and learn."

* * * *

Wilfred and Bubba cleaned their weapons and got their gear ready. Wilfred asked, "You think the Caller will show up?"

Bubba nodded. "Yeah."

"Do you think Dix and Petersen will catch him?"

"I think so. They seem pretty sharp. Why?"

Wilfred looked at his brother. "The asshole's been up to no good for so long, it seems a little farfetched he'd get caught so easily. We've done as much as we can to identify the guy. I say we just post ourselves near the storage unit and wait until someone tries to steal the cocaine."

Bubba agreed.

Wilfred said, "I know we told Dix we'd stay out of the way, but I want to take the guy out myself. We know just as much as they do, and we should be in on the action. I know we're not cops, but we shouldn't have to sit on the sidelines."

Bubba looked up and smiled. "I'm with you."

"So what do we do?"

"Sit and wait." Bubba chambered a round in his sidearm.

Wilfred thought out loud. "They believe the Caller's coming in a day or two. I think he's been in on the investigation since it started, and I bet he'll try to take the stuff tonight."

"Why's dat?"

Wilfred continued. "The longer he waits, the more resources will be deployed against him. Striking quickly would make it easier to grab the load and get out."

Bubba rubbed his chin. "You think he'll come by plane, car, or helicopter? What?"

"We can probably rule out planes and helicopters. They're too big and can easily be tracked. The guy'll show up with some serious heat, storm the storage unit with a large van or SUV, load up, and drive away. The only questions left are where would he go after that, and how he would get his haul off the island undetected?"

Bubba shrugged.

They loaded their gear into their rundown hatchback. Books, magazines, a small handheld police scanner, and whatever else they could think of might help pass the time. Then they headed to the storage unit.

As they drove past the airport to check out the jet the Coast Guard honcho was supposed to have arrived in, they saw the plane and the horse head and decided to stick around. They watched through binoculars as a white guy unloaded what appeared to be weapons into the back of a Yukon Denali. They found it odd because a second Yukon Denali was parked near the first one, but the man wasn't doing anything with it. They had never seen the man, the jet, or the SUV before.

After each movement, the guy looked around. Wilfred thought he saw small round objects across the man's chest.

He turned to Bubba. "Look through these binoculars.

You think those are grenades on his chest?"

Bubba took the binoculars, stared, and sighed. "Maybe."

They watched as the man unloaded a shotgun with a bright, orange barrel.

Bubba passed the binoculars back to Wilfred.

"You see da shotgun with an orange barrel? What does dat mean?"

"Less-than-lethal. It shoots bean bag rounds."

As the man leaned over, his shirt lifted slightly, exposing a sidearm on his hip. Wilfred spotted a tattoo on the guy's upper arm when he took off his coat. He wasn't sure but thought it looked a lot like a Special Forces Operational Detachment-Delta (Airborne) insignia. It was the same tattoo Wilfred's cousin had on his arm.

Wilfred looked through his binoculars and focused on the red horse head on the rear of the plane. He passed the binoculars to Bubba and pointed. His brother looked and then gave him a thumbs-up. It was definitely the same horse head on the cocaine Wilfred had located.

"We should stick with this guy." Bubba nodded.

They ducked low in the car and kept watch. About two hours later, another plane landed, and it looked very similar to the one they'd been watching. It too had a red horse emblem. *This operation continues getting very interesting*, thought Wilfred.

CHAPTER FORTY

Jorge Blanco sped to Goldfinger's, a local Miami strip club, where his partners hung out. None of his men, who were supposedly on standby, had answered calls. As he pulled into the parking lot, he located Paul Kemp's Chevy Suburban. *Well, at least I know they're here.*

He jumped from the cab of his truck and strolled to the entrance. A very large black man stood in front of the door with his arms folded. He scowled.

Blanco walked closer. "Hello. How are you? I need to find a few friends."

The bouncer replied, "Can't let you in. It's a VIP club tonight, and I don't know you, so you ain't getting in."

"Maybe you know my friends." He pointed over to the Suburban. "They came in that."

"I know 'em, but I ain't seen you. They busy right now. When they done, I'll check with 'em. Otherwise, you ain't gettin' in tonight, partner."

What a bunch of horseshit. "Listen, pal, what's it going to take to get me inside?"

The guy looked him up and down, then shrugged. "A couple hundred."

Blanco stepped within two feet of the guy and pretended to get his wallet out. While the guy was distracted, Blanco placed him firmly in a choke hold. The bouncer tried to release himself by smashing Blanco against the outside of the building, but Blanco held on, and the bouncer fell to the ground. The big man was asleep within seconds. Without further interruption, Blanco let himself in.

Scanning the tables and lap-dance couches he didn't see his team. *Damn. What are those idiots doing now?*

He approached the bartender and asked her if she'd seen four white guys wearing cargo pants and polo shirts come in together. She said she had and they were in the back room. Blanco thanked her and started to walk toward the rear of the club. He hoped whatever the men were doing wasn't completely illegal. If they were late for their mission, his ass would be on the line.

The door to the back room was locked and felt pretty solid. After he had knocked loudly a couple of times, Blanco decided to force entry.

Efforts to kick and shoulder the door were unsuccessful. Without hesitation, he pulled out his .45 caliber Sig Sauer and put a few rounds through the lock. People ran for cover and screamed, but Blanco remained calm. The door was shattered and Blanco stepped inside. What he saw made him wish he had never become involved with the operation or the DOG Unit.

His men were engaged in various sexual activities, interrupted only by the gunfire. Lines of cocaine and piles of cash lay on the table, and empty bottles of whiskey littered the floor.

Blanco shook his head. "What in the hell are you shitheads doing? Get your goddamn clothes on, put your fucking weapons away, and get the hell out of here."

They did as they were told. Blanco turned to the women. "All right, ladies, your orgy got a little out of hand. How much cash will it take to make this go away?"

None of them responded.

"Listen, I don't have time to stick around. What's it going to take to make you forget these guys were ever here?"

One of the strippers said, "Give us ten thousand in cash, and it never happened."

Blanco chuckled. "How much did they already pay you?" "About four thousand."

Reaching into his pocket, he pulled out a wad of cash. He counted out sixty one-hundred dollar bills and put the money on the table.

He looked at the women. "If I hear one thing about tonight's party, I'll kill everyone in here and burn the place to the ground. No one will find your bodies, and they won't catch me."

Blanco went outside and saw the bouncer talking to his team near Kemp's vehicle.

The bouncer spotted Blanco and pointed. "You motherfucker. I'm gonna kill you."

He reached for his .38 special at his waist, but the gun was gone.

Blanco pulled the guy's firearm from his own waistband. "Looking for this?" He disabled the weapon and threw it across the parking lot. "Next time, I'll kill you."

He ordered the team into their vehicle, and they sped away. Blanco calculated they could still deploy to the Bahamas on schedule. Blanco was about to give the team the *what for* speech when his cell phone rang.

Tony Charles said, "There's been a change of plans. The unit will continue to Andros Island. However, you need to meet Jim Calhoun to assist him with an operation involving a hundred million dollar load of cocaine he's trying to protect from corrupt local cops. Calhoun is already on the island. I'm sending you all the intel we have on the situation. Calhoun will give you instructions when your boots are on the ground."

These guys couldn't possibly screw up a simple mission, could they? Blanco was beside himself.

He advised his men of the change in plans. Barely over an hour later, they were in the air, headed for the Bahamas.

CHAPTER FORTY-ONE

When Roger stopped the car in front of the restaurant, Dix jumped out hoping to ask Calhoun about the plane before they got inside and started drinking. *There's no telling what I might say to this pompous jerk if I was buzzed.*

He couldn't figure how a guy making his salary could afford a forty million dollar plane. The Coast Guard had probably seized it, but he was also baffled why the same horse head from the narcotics was on the side of the plane.

Calhoun exited the vehicle with Commissioner Knowles.

Dix corralled him. "How does a guy on your salary get to fly around in such an expensive plane? Did you write the expenditure off in the Deepwater proposal?"

Calhoun smiled. "Don't you read the newspaper? We seized the plane at Miami International last year during a drug interdiction. It belonged to one of the biggest dealers in Columbia. Unfortunately, he wasn't on it at the time, just a bunch of his mules."

"So the Coast Guard gets to fly around in seized property like that? What if the owner came looking for it?"

Calhoun raised an eyebrow. "I suppose it's a possibility, but highly unlikely. He'd need a legitimate reason to get the plane back and prove he purchased it without using drug money. We needed to get here quick. It was the best option. All the cutters headed out before I could catch a ride. I asked to use the plane, and the grownups okayed it."

Dix wasn't finished. "I see all the USGC stuff on the plane, but why the small red horse head logo?"

Calhoun chuckled. "That's my own punch to the gut, directed at the plane's owner. For years, I've been chasing a supplier using the same red horse head stamped on the kilos he produces. I know it comes out of Columbia, but I lose track of it until we find it in the Caribbean or in Miami. I left the horse there so if he sees it, he'll be pissed the Coast Guard is riding around in his forty million dollar toy."

Petersen stepped closer. "The cocaine in the storage facility has the same exact marking on it."

Calhoun looked surprised. "You're shittin' me. Damn. Now I'm even more interested in this case. You guys have been hunting my bad guy for a few days. I've been looking for him for twenty years."

He stepped back and looked thoughtful. "I heard about him when I was still in Special Ops. When he sees his plane here, he's going to shit. The guy is aggressive and won't let this load get away."

Dix motioned to the restaurant. "Gentlemen, what say we grab a bite to eat?"

Except for a few of the local officers who stood guard outside, they entered and ordered appetizers and well drinks. Calhoun ordered lots of rounds.

Dix wondered if Calhoun was for real. Maybe the guy intended to get the men drunk to keep them off-balance when he came to take the cocaine. Too much about Calhoun didn't set right with Dix. He just didn't trust the guy.

* * * *

Calhoun glanced at his Rolex GMT-Master II and calculated in about six hours, he and his son would be safely airborne with his shipment and headed to Canada.

He continued to order the men as many drinks as it took to get them drunk, which he hoped would render enough of them useless.

Most seemed unaffected by the alcohol. They were supposed to be on duty, but Calhoun was impressed by how eager they were to spend his money. Since the commissioner was downing drinks with his men, he apparently condoned such behavior.

After several more rounds and the appetizers, the men appeared lethargic and intoxicated. Commissioner Knowles excused most of the locals and told them to go home to get some rest.

Dix asked Roger to take him and Petersen back to the lodge, and all three left.

Calhoun remained with a few local officers who appeared too drunk to drive. He'd tried to squeeze more information out of them with cash, but he couldn't find any takers.

After everyone had found rides, Calhoun pulled out his cell phone to call his son. He hit the speed dial and got voicemail. *That's odd. Maybe the phone's turned off. But he knows better than that.*

Commissioner Knowles emerged from the men's room and offered Calhoun a ride.

Calhoun smiled. "No, thank you, sir. I'll have my pilot pick me up here shortly. Thanks for the offer."

"Not a problem, Mr. Calhoun. Call me if you need anything."

As the guy walked away, Calhoun had a moment of regret. He was going to embarrass the hell out of the commissioner in a few short hours. *Maybe I'll send him a postcard from the Seychelles when it's over.* Nope, never leave clues.

CHAPTER FORTY-TWO

The DOG Unit arrived on schedule at the Mangrove Cay Airport on Andros Island at eighteen hundred hours. They met their contact standing next to a black Yukon Denali. Blanco, Lester, and Kemp didn't know much about the guy, except he never seemed to be far from Lieutenant Commander Jim Calhoun.

Blanco offered his hand, and the guy shook it.

"Can you fill us in on the new objectives?"

"Certainly." He unrolled underground schematics for the area beneath the storage yard where the narcotics were locked up and pointed to a specific spot. "Under here is a series of tunnels. They're apparently not guarded and have been overlooked by the locals. Between the top of the tunnel and the floor is approximately five feet of clay, dirt, and concrete. We need to get a heavy duty vehicle underneath, drill a hole large enough for two bodies to get through and retrieve the drugs."

Blanco considered asking Lester or Kemp how this should go down since they had expertise in concrete work, but they were busy throwing up. The other two members of his team were drinking Gatorade and eating Snickers bars.

Blanco shook his head. "Exactly what are we going to do after we get inside?"

"You have to avoid detection and retrieve approximately twelve hundred and fifty kilos in large black duffel bags, locked in a cabinet near the boat. The locals were not advised of the details because the Coast Guard and DEA believe some of them are corrupt and are plotting to take the stuff themselves."

"I assume after we retrieve the duffel bags, we place them in the armored transport and drive them back here?"

The contact nodded. "Correct."

"Then what? And what do we do if we're detected?"

The guy looked stern. "You're paid to be untraceable and work undetected. However, should that occur, complete the mission at any cost."

"That means taking out cops?" Blanco was skeptical.

Without hesitation the man said, "Affirmative. Once the narcotics are brought to the tarmac, you and your men will help me load them into this jet." He smacked the tail section with his hand, "Then, you guys go one way, and the Lieutenant Commander and I go another."

"You mean the Coast Guard wants this dope so bad it's authorizing the use of deadly force against cops? This smells dirty. Unless Calhoun confirms the order, we won't proceed." Blanco had heard enough.

The contact scowled. "The men guarding the cocaine are corrupt and have ties with the Caller. We've brought along some non-lethal options to incapacitate them long enough for you to get on your way. But, if push comes to shove, you may have to kill them."

Blanco remained skeptical. "When I hear it from Calhoun himself, we'll continue. This sounds like a training mission to me. Where's the armored vehicle you were talking about?"

"You're standing next to it. That Denali has been outfitted as a highly mobile, miniature tank. Small arms fire won't penetrate the skin, and spike strips are useless. We hope no one will know the narcotics are gone until we're all clear. Should the situation get hot, a Stingray Helicopter will be on standby status just north of the tarmac. Proceed to the helicopter, unload the duffel bags, and get the hell out of here."

Blanco still didn't like the sound of the mission. It didn't make sense. He and his team were not going to take out cops, regardless of how dirty they were supposed to be. Speaking to Jim Calhoun was now imperative, and soon.

The team inspected the equipment in the back of the Denali. They agreed it was sufficient to complete the objective, should they continue. They got their gear on, loaded the weapons and jumped in the SUV to wait for orders from Calhoun.

As he started the vehicle, Blanco looked back at the contact. "You coming?"

"Nope. You guys are the experts. I'm just a lowly assistant. Mr. Calhoun will contact you in approximately five minutes with the final orders. I know you don't need it, but good luck."

The men headed for the access point to the underground tunnels. Exactly as predicted, Blanco got a call from Calhoun while they were on the way.

Calhoun said, "Blanco, you're exactly right. This is a training mission, nothing more. We made it as real as we could, but obviously I don't want anyone to get hurt."

Blanco felt better. "So there isn't a hundred million dollars of cocaine in the warehouse right?"

Calhoun never skipped a beat. "Of course not."

Blanco was miffed that it was only a training mission, but he felt much better knowing he'd sniffed it out. "Copy that, sir."

* * * *

Wilfred and Bubba had never fought in a war, but they understood street warfare, where those who were the smartest and quickest to react tended to live longest. When the second plane landed at the airport, they cringed. Five guys deplaned and surveyed the surroundings while taking defensive positions. Each man was armed with an M16 rifle. Once they seemed satisfied, there were no immediate threats, they covered each other as they made their way to a man standing beside the Denali.

Bubba figured the guy who seemed to be doing most of the talking was the leader of the new group that had just arrived.

Wilfred and Bubba took turns looking through the binoculars trying to gather as much information as they could in the hopes of relaying it to Roger, Dix, and Petersen. They watched as the pilot produced papers that resembled schematics they'd seen. The pilot and the other men huddled over them.

As two of the new arrivals began to vomit, Bubba chuckled. "Dem boys don't look so good. Two of 'em just threw up."

Wilfred was concerned. "They look serious and ready for action to me and with those heavy weapons, they look mean as hell. The pilot for the Coast Guard bigwig is showing them equipment, but I can't figure out what it is or what it would be used for."

Bubba took the binoculars. "Looks like someone's gonna work on concrete. But I'm not sure. One of those things looks like a monster drill."

While Wilfred took the binoculars, Bubba called one of his friends who worked construction on the islands. Bubba described what he'd seen.

"My buddy says it could be masonry drilling equipment, based on the size and type of bit."

Wilfred looked at his brother. "What would they need drilling tools for? This shit gets stranger with every minute. These have to be the guys we thought would come to get the cocaine. I say we follow them. I bet they'll lead us to the Caller."

Bubba agreed, so they hunkered down in the hopes of getting a piece of the action later.

The newcomers checked their watches, talked for a few more minutes and loaded the black SUV with gear from the plane. Then they headed off the tarmac while the pilot remained with the jet.

As soon as the SUV was out of view, the pilot made a phone call that lasted less than ten seconds. He hung up, retrieved an M16 rifle from the jet and slung it over his shoulder. He lit a cigarette and slowly inhaled.

Bubba turned to Wilfred. "That pilot isn't going anywhere. Let's follow the dudes in the big SUV."

Wilfred turned the key. "Okay. I'll drive. Keep an eye on them."

Bubba sulked. "Why don't I drive?"

Wilfred looked at his brother. "Man, you already wore out the springs on this side. Our tires wouldn't last ten miles if you drove. Besides, you're a better observer. Tell me where to go."

Bubba acquiesced. "Next street, turn right. We'll run parallel to 'em for a bit."

They hadn't discussed what they'd do if they actually confronted the bastard who ordered the hit on Sean and Preston. Bubba locked and loaded their weapons and set out the extra magazines. At a red light, they donned their vests and slipped on their game faces.

Staying several car lengths behind the Denali, they drove about eight miles without saying a word. Their target vehicle stayed precisely at the speed limit and stopped at all the stop signs and the lone signal. It made a series of right-hand turns followed by a couple of left turns.

After ten long minutes, Wilfred broke the silence. "I don't think these guys are going directly to the storage yard. In fact, it looks like they're headed about four miles south of it. You got any idea where they might be going?" Before he let Bubba answer,

Wilfred asked another question. "You think maybe we got this wrong?"

Bubba watched the Denali intently. The car had stopped near a flimsy chain-link fence, and the guy in the right front passenger seat got out. With a pair of large bolt cutters, he cut the padlock, swung the gate open, and got back in the vehicle. After the SUV had pulled in, the left rear passenger got out to secure the gate.

Bubba pointed. "Dey stopped and went in there. I lost 'em after that."

Wilfred grimaced. "We have to be a few miles south of the storage unit. There's too much firepower and too many men in that SUV to just be driving around aimlessly. Where the hell did they go?"

Bubba had already pulled out his phone. He dialed a number and waited. His granddaddy knew the island better than anyone.

CHAPTER FORTY-THREE

Three of the names on Snead's list were eliminated by midnight through a series of phone calls and searches. They'd also been questioned and threatened with polygraphs. Each person welcomed the polygraph and said they had nothing to hide.

Snead shook his head. The only name left on his list was Rear Admiral Tony Charles.

That was unofficial. Officially, there was one more name with a red line already through it: Lieutenant Commander Jim Calhoun.

Snead wrestled with the name for several minutes and began to sift through his data and leads. Most everything pointed to Tony Charles, but that was because he hadn't considered Jim Calhoun. He couldn't believe the guy could have anything to do with drug trafficking.

If it weren't for the fact that he was getting nowhere with connecting Tony Charles to the Caller, he wouldn't have considered inserting Calhoun into the equation. He felt almost guilty even considering it, but it was his last resort.

He was concerned for Dix and Petersen and assumed they were in real trouble. He figured he owed it to them to consider every angle.

Snead considered the timelines and events from when he first met Jim Calhoun. They were both recently out of the service and trying to become cops. About thirty years ago they'd both applied to Miami-Dade PD. Both were accepted and gainfully employed until Calhoun was caught having a relationship with another officer's wife.

Calhoun was told to resign or be fired. None of the men on the force at that time was still around. The whole event had been swept under the rug as Calhoun grudgingly resigned.

Then, somehow the guy ended up with the Coast Guard. He rose through the ranks quickly and developed a reputation for catching drug smugglers in the Atlantic and the Caribbean. He earned the nickname 'the Bloodhound,' taught narcotics training for the FBI at Quantico and held seminars on the topic all around the United States. Calhoun ate, slept, and breathed narcotics and was possibly the greatest expert in the country.

Snead realized the type of drug smuggler he was looking for would need that type of expertise to be successful. Calhoun might actually be the guy everyone was looking for. He reluctantly included him as a suspect. As he pieced the facts together on the timeline he'd created, Snead grew more upset. *How did I miss this?* The name of the registered owner of the speedboat, access to the computer used to register the vessel, and the timeframe of his career, all the circumstantial evidence pointed to Calhoun, not Charles.

Snead recalled the trouble his contacts were having trying to search through internet databases and remembered Calhoun had attended MIT for two years when he'd become bored. Everywhere he looked, fragments of the puzzle pointed at Calhoun, but not enough to develop probable cause for a search warrant, let alone a strong case for conviction.

While he contemplated more options and other ways to link Calhoun to the case, he had an epiphany. He needed to run his idea by Dix and Petersen immediately and was looking for his cell phone when he heard it ring. He picked it up, looked at his caller ID, and realized it was Dix. *Does this guy have great timing or what?*

Snead answered. "Buddy, am I glad to hear from you."

Dix jumped right in. "You won't believe this, but your friend Jim Calhoun arrived on the island in a Lear jet. To top it off, on the side of the jet is a red horse head, just like the one on the cocaine over here. He says he seized it from a Colombian drug lord and left the horse head on the plane to piss off the guy."

Snead thought that odd. "And he arrived on the same jet?"

"Yep."

"Wow, he's got to have huge clout to be flying around in a seized piece of property worth upwards of forty million. Interesting."

Dix detected some sarcasm. "Why don't you sound surprised?"

"That's because I'm not. I've been getting the same sense here. It still doesn't feel right saying it, but too many things point to my old friend, Jim Calhoun. I don't like it, but right now everyone is a suspect. My investigation suggests the person you're looking for may have handled dozens of murders and missing persons over the years. He's not someone to take lightly."

Dix was caught off guard. "Wait. You mean to tell me you actually think Calhoun is the Caller?"

Snead continued, "It seems Calhoun owns a few pieces of expensive property and some toys that are unreported, some under pseudonyms. All together, we're looking at about six to seven million dollars in net worth. Even if he'd invested very wisely, I don't think he would be able to afford those things on the salary he makes. And he takes a lot of expensive vacations."

"So he has a great portfolio. But how does that make him the Caller?"

"I've thought about the name on the speedboat registration and how the transaction was completed. Calhoun is connected to both of them. I hate to say this, but can you think of anyone else who would know more about the Caribbean drug trade than Calhoun? I can't. He also has access to UAVs and had input over the years on where the cutters would patrol. All he'd have to do was send the birds and the boats away from his shipments, and they'd get through. It would explain the tremendous success rate of your bad guy."

Dix was silent for a moment. "Snead, I've known you a long time. You know I respect the shit out of you but are we stretching this a little too far? I mean, I'm not crazy about the guy, but come on, the Bloodhound as our drug smuggler and killer?"

"Listen, Dix, I don't want it to be true, either. Most of it is circumstantial evidence, but you have to consider Calhoun as a suspect. What we've found all leads back to him. The guy's on the island right now helping devise a plan to capture a bad guy, your bad guy. If *he's* the bad guy, he'll do everything he can to learn everyone else's plans, develop one to allow him to grab the dope, and be off the island before anyone, including you, has any idea what happened. He's got the expertise, the resources, and the need to get that coke back. If I had to guess, I'd say he'll probably move tonight, not in a few days."

"Okay, I'll keep him under close surveillance. Petersen and I are headed to the storage yard. If I hear anything, I'll get back to you. And if you find something concrete to tie Calhoun to all of this, something I can put in a report and prove in court, let me know." Dix was still doubtful.

Snead hung up, shook his mouse to wake his computer and began searching for more clues.

CHAPTER FORTY-FOUR

Pierce put one of his best interrogators, Keith O'Reilly, to work on the dealer they'd apprehended with the search warrant. O'Reilly was a brutal tactician. He'd tried every angle to solicit information.

O'Reilly had gotten tiny pieces of information but nothing concrete. The moment the dealer was arrested, he'd asked for a cigarette. No one had given him one. Since the interrogation was stagnant, O'Reilly requested a pack and placed them on the table. The dealer finally broke his silence. "I was on the phone with a guy I know as the Caller. The cops were breaking down my door. They had a search warrant."

"Who is the Caller?"

The dealer eyed the pack of cigarettes on the table between them. "I don't know, man. He works for either the Coast Guard or the navy. He's been running drugs for a long time."

O'Reilly didn't give him a cigarette.

"Come on, man. I told you what I know. Just one. I gotta have one."

"Not until you give up something useful. How do you know he works for the Coast Guard or navy?"

The dealer guy hesitated. "I did three transactions with him face-to-face."

O'Reilly gave him one cigarette, but no lighter or match. The guy promptly chewed the cigarette and swallowed it. The dealer looked relieved. "How about another one?"

O'Reilly shook his head. "Describe the man you worked with so we can put together a photo lineup. If you positively identify the subject, you'll get the cigarettes and a lighter. What you do and say from here on out will determine if you walk away or spend your life in prison."

The dealer's head dropped. "Anything, anything you want, just give me a fucking cigarette, man, please. The guy is white, muscular. I'd say he's in his fifties by now. He always smoked cigars when we did business, and I heard someone call him 'Hound' something."

The room froze. O'Reilly looked at the two-way mirror. He knew Pierce and two of his guys stood behind the glass. Everyone wondered if the drug dealer was talking about 'Bloodhound,' a nickname for Jim Calhoun, a high ranking member of the US Coast Guard, and an internationally known narcotic expert.

Pierce decided to relieve O'Reilly. But before he could get to the interrogation room, his phone rang. It was a call from Snead.

After Snead's update, Pierce had to agree, Jim Calhoun, was likely the Caller. Pierce told Snead about the dealer's stunning revelation. "I want the dope dealer to positively identify the guy he knew as the Caller and the 'Hound.' Make sure they are the same person."

"Call me back either way. I'll let Dix and Petersen know. But we still need hard evidence before we can bring Calhoun in for questioning. And we need to be damn sure of our facts or our asses will be roasted on a spit."

Snead hung up, and Pierce entered the room to further question the drug dealer.

Ten minutes later, photographs of several people, all matching the dealer's general description of the 'Hound,' were laid out on the table in front of the guy. He looked at the photos and when he got to one of Jim Calhoun, he glanced away.

Pierce noticed the reaction. "You're looking at life in prison. Can you point out the guy or not?"

Without hesitation, the dealer pointed to the picture of Lieutenant Commander Jim Calhoun. "That's the guy."

"Are you sure?" Pierce wanted no mistakes.

"Yep. Positive."

"That's the guy you know as the Caller and 'Hound?'" The dealer looked up, defeated. "Yeah, and I'm probably a dead man walking now."

Pierce stood up and ordered cigarettes and a lighter for the suspect.

The news of the positive identification spread quickly through the team.

Pierce grew serious. "Lock it up, guys. We've just started this one. We'll need more hard evidence to make this stick in court. Calhoun won't go easily, especially if he knows we're looking for him. Tell no one what we're doing."

Next he contacted his superior and requested he and his team be allowed to fly to Andros immediately to help Dix and Petersen apprehend Jim Calhoun. His supervisor wanted every single piece of evidence tying Calhoun to the case before considering him as a suspect. After an intense debriefing, the Chief ordered Pierce and his guys to Andros.

Pierce quickly called Snead.

Snead didn't hesitate. "It's him, right?"

"The dealer has concrete evidence connecting Calhoun to the Caller, and he positively identified Calhoun in a photo lineup. He even said someone referred to the Caller as the 'Hound.' We're headed out as soon as possible to Andros. Are you coming?"

Snead grabbed his keys and started for his car. "You're damn right. I wouldn't miss this rodeo. I'll meet you at the airport. I never thought I'd see anything like it in my lifetime, but all I really care about is getting to Dix and Petersen before the Bloodhound does.

CHAPTER FORTY-FIVE

Bubba slowly explained his exact location to his grandfather but never took his eyes off the gated fence. He'd called his grandfather, assuming the old man might know something about the place he and Wilfred lost sight of the SUV. They were locked and loaded, but he hoped they'd never have to use their weapons. Bubba figured the men they'd been watching were well-trained and had significant firepower.

His grandfather hesitated. "Sounds as though you're at the entrance to the old underground tunnels."

Bubba looked at Wilfred in surprise. "What underground tunnels?" Wilfred raised an eyebrow, and Bubba held up his hand for silence.

"As best I recall, those tunnels were used for repairs to utilities and such. But they started caving in, so they were closed up, maybe forty years ago."

Bubba was worried. "Where do they go?"

His grandfather laughed. "Why, all over through the center of the town, I'd guess."

"Do you know the place where the police store stuff?"

"You talking about the warehouse?"

"Yes. Do the tunnels go under there?"

The old man paused. "I was down there years ago. Don't remember for sure, but they probably do. Seems like they went all over. But some caved in. Don't know exactly where they go today."

Bubba smiled. "Thanks, Pops."

He whistled and turned to Wilfred. "Man, Granddaddy thinks this is the way to some old tunnels that could still lead under the warehouse."

Wilfred looked stunned. "I don't recall anyone talking about tunnels under the city."

Bubba quickly dialed Dix's number. No answer. He tried Petersen with the same result, so he tried Dix again.

Bubba stared at his phone. He finally had something useful for Dix and no way of sharing it with him.

Wilfred raised an eyebrow. "Well, do we stay here or follow those guys? What do you think we should do?"

"I'll keep calling Dix. You continue trying Petersen. Then I say we just sit and watch. I don't know where them dudes went, but we ain't leaving."

After five minutes of repeated calling, they both gave up. Wilfred shook his head. "We have to follow those guys. They already have a long head start. If we don't go now, we may not find them in time. Call your granddaddy back and see if this is the only way in or out."

Bubba punched in the number and asked his grandfather Wilfred's question.

"Like I said, it's been a long time. But I think there's only one way in."

Bubba thanked the old man again and hung up. "This is it."

They tried reaching Dix or Petersen again with no success.

Wilfred opened his door. "I'd sure feel better if I knew we had backup."

"Yeah or if someone else knew where we are." Bubba opened his own door.

Wilfred said, "We don't know the layout of the tunnels, and it's been about thirty minutes since those guys went inside. We could probably take them out with the element of surprise on our side, but I sure wish we knew where we were going."

As Bubba eased himself out of the passenger seat, his phone rang.

The incoming call was from Roger.

CHAPTER FORTY-SIX

The members of the DOG Unit worked efficiently and quietly. They were beneath the target and about a third of the way through the clay and rebar searching for the four-to-six inches of concrete of the warehouse floor. Blanco had been ordered to send a text message to Calhoun when they were ready to grab the narcotics. This would let Calhoun know it was time to disable the APS and cripple the surveillance equipment, creating a diversion.

Thirty-four minutes later, the drilling equipment finally broke through the warehouse floor.

Using a snake camera the size of a pen cap, Blanco examined the area closely. About fifty yards north of the speedboat, two Royal Bahamian Police Force officers watched the area. On each side of the facility, two more officers stood guard, making a total of six. But he knew there were probably more not far away. Blanco moved the tiny camera around to locate the cabinet containing the targeted duffel bags. He located it on the second pass.

Most of the guards he could see from his vantage point appeared to be out of shape and tired. He watched as a couple rubbed their eyes and shook their heads as if trying to stay awake. The team's orders were to get in, retrieve the bags, and get out undetected. Blanco planned to do it all, and not have to fire a single round. He considered the dirty cops. *Someone else can deal with them.*

Blanco and Kemp continued drilling to create enough space to place small elongated C4 charges. The plan was to ignite them once the diversion was created by Calhoun. To prevent the large slabs of concrete from dropping to the floor below, a series of anchors were strategically placed and a large mesh net was positioned around the drilled and prepped opening into the warehouse. The team gave each other thumbs up indicating they were set.

Blanco texted Calhoun. The team prepared themselves to remove the concrete, enter the warehouse, and retrieve the duffel bags.

Right on schedule, the lights, surveillance cameras, and audio feeds went dead as Calhoun snapped the lock off the APS unit and disabled the main power line with bolt cutters. Shortly afterward, Blanco pressed the switch to ignite the C4 to dislodge the concrete to gain access to the warehouse. The pieces slid into the tunnels amidst dust from the detonation. One piece fell out of the safety net making a strong thud sound. Blanco popped his head out of the hole swiftly to see what was happening in the warehouse. Through night-vision goggles, Blanco saw the officers trying to get oriented in the warehouse, now without light. He watched as one ran directly toward him. Next to him, Timms popped his head up, picked up the same threat and downed the man with a beanbag round before he got too close. The guard was struck in the chest and lay motionless.

Blanco whispered, "Shit."

Timms whispered back, "So much for stealth."

Timms and Blanco quickly brought up 40 mm launchers and shot smoke grenades and flash-bang grenades into the warehouse. This disoriented the remaining officers and made a little cushion of open space around the speedboat.

With their night-vision goggles in place, the team entered the warehouse and scrambled to access the cabinet. They broke the lock and began unloading the duffel bags. They slid them to the holes in the warehouse floor and pushed the bags into the holes. When all bags were below, the team followed back into the tunnels. Once in the tunnels, the DOG Unit worked feverishly to get the cocaine into the Denali.

Six minutes later, the fatigued team members climbed into the Yukon and sped back the way they'd come through the tunnels.

Blanco finally allowed himself to breathe. "I'm extremely proud of you guys. So far, there are no casualties and we're on schedule." *I sure need to work out more. I'm completely winded.*

Timms said, "Man, that was almost too easy. I heard a bunch of yelling and screaming, but no firing. We were met with little resistance, except the one guy I dropped with the bean bag round. None of the guards came to see what exactly was going on."

He paused. "Something isn't right. I get the feeling they wanted us to get away with the dope. You think this was just a training mission?"

Blanco calculated the situation. Right now, all he knew was he had duffel bags of suspected cocaine in the Yukon. As far as he knew, this was just a training mission. His mind began to play tricks with him. *What if Calhoun just played us?*

He realized no one checked the bags to see what was actually inside. Blanco slammed on the brakes. *Son of a bitch.* He jumped out and ran toward the rear of the Yukon.

Blanco smiled and looked at his team. "Guys, relax. Timms called it. This was another training mission."

Timms responded, "Then why'd we stop? And why are you ripping open that duffel bag?"

Blanco didn't pay attention to Timms. He frantically opened the sealed duffel bag with his knife. White powder poured from the side. *Oh shit. I wonder if that's cocaine.*

He shook his head. "I'm not going to bullshit you. We may have a major problem here." He pointed at the white powder pouring out of the duffel bag he'd ripped. "That may be pure cocaine. If it is, we just opened up a serious can of worms."

The team members looked at each other then back at Blanco.

He continued, "For argument's sake, let's assume…" The thud in his chest from the bean bag round knocked him to the ground. Blanco's head hit the tunnel floor as unconsciousness claimed him.

The rest of the team looked at Timms, who held a less-than-lethal shotgun. "What? He was about to figure out we're working for Calhoun and we just stole a shit load of cocaine from local police." Timms threw the shotgun behind him and pulled out his sidearm.

He walked over to finish off Blanco.

Kemp jumped between Timms and Blanco's body. "Stealing cocaine for a big payday is one thing. Killing Blanco is another." He looked at the rest of the team and then back at Timms. "We aren't killing Blanco. You guys got us sucked into Calhoun's trap and we all need the money. But, a murder case of a fellow unit member is bullshit and something neither of us needs."

Timms was pissed and wanted to finish off Blanco. "Just because Calhoun put him in charge, doesn't mean I won't kill him. There's a reason Blanco wasn't included in this part of the plan. He's weak and he'll spend the rest of his life looking for us after he learns what we did."

Kemp agreed Blanco was weak but pointed at Timms and the rest of the men. "Get in the car and drive. We're behind schedule now. End of discussion."

Timms hesitantly got into the driver's seat as the other members filed in. They sped away, leaving Blanco lying in the tunnel.

Kemp kept his eyes on Timms as they neared the tunnel entrance. He clicked the Bluetooth in his ear and dialed the boss. Calhoun needed to know the mission might have been compromised. However, the concrete and steel in the tunnels made it impossible for Kemp's call to get through at that moment.

* * * *

As planned, Calhoun left the storage yard after causing orchestrated chaos. He casually worked his way back to the airport in a rental car his son had obtained and delivered earlier in the evening when everyone was out drinking. He'd parked the car a few blocks from the APS and left an assault rifle and ballistic vest under the passenger seat. There was also a change of clothes.

He had no idea if the DOG Unit had been successful or if they'd had to kill anyone. Since he hadn't heard from Blanco or Kemp, he figured everything was okay. He realized playing Blanco against Kemp by not letting him in on the secret was a risk. But, he needed Blanco's brains and leadership. Then it hit him. Calhoun began to wonder if things, in fact, had gone too easily. Not knowing the status of the cocaine really bothered him. He considered ditching the rental car and taking the small Cessna he'd had moved to the small, unimproved runway along the south end of the island.

Calhoun chuckled. *You're overreacting.* Greed forced him to believe everything was fine, and he contemplated ways to spend all his money once his buyer paid for the cocaine. He was confident it was still untraceable, but replaying what had just occurred at the storage facility made him start to worry again. Things were going as planned, but he remained anxious to get out of the country.

Taking the pre-planned route from the APS to the main airport, he was cautious of people on the street, on bikes, or in vehicles. He was weary of the locals as well since he assumed the men on his payroll had been hauled in and may have provided investigators with information point them in his direction. The constant worry about his secret identity consumed Calhoun. He just couldn't be sure he was still in the clear. Before he had a chance to test the theory, he made a right turn and saw two local police vehicles coming right at him. Their emergency lights were spinning and the sirens were blaring. Calhoun's heart seemed to stop from nerves. It was an feeling he hadn't had in a long time. Now was definitely not the time for this to happen.

He frantically looked for a way to dodge the local police cars. Buildings lined the street. No alleys. In a matter of seconds they would be on him. Calhoun saw a parked car and maneuvered his vehicle behind it so he could use the vehicle's engine compartment as cover when he opened fire.

The aggressive maneuver got the attention of the two policemen who had no knowledge that Calhoun was the Caller. As they braked hard to investigate, Calhoun popped up and riddled their cars with high-velocity rounds. The police vehicles and officers were shredded. Calhoun was no stranger to dead bodies. He believed the ones in front of him were clearly dead but scanned the area for further threats and detected none.

He slammed on the accelerator and drove directly to the airport. He still wasn't sure if the locals or the Miami detectives were on to him, but he'd just murdered two cops. He assumed someone must have witnessed it. As soon as he could, Calhoun was going to get the hell off the island.

* * * *

Bubba called two of his friends who were dump truck operators on Andros Island. They agreed to bring their big vehicles to the tunnel entrance and block it, in case they needed to stop the suspects.

He then phoned Roger back. Putting his phone on speaker, he asked Roger to put Dix on. When he answered, Bubba told him, "Mon, we got a situation here." He quickly relayed what they'd seen. Wilfred nodded his agreement.

"How did we miss something like that? Do you guys have a visual on the men in the SUV? All hell broke loose at the warehouse."

Bubba replied, "We watched them go through the gate. I called Pops, my grandfather. He said there were underground utility tunnels throughout the city. This is the entrance. The guys haven't come out yet, but everything went black a few minutes ago. We figured there must have been an attack at the warehouse."

"Tunnels. Why didn't someone tell us about them? Christ, it's too late to focus on that now. Listen, we have a lot of evidence indicating Calhoun is the Caller. We need to catch him trying to leave with the drugs to cement the case against him."

This time Wilfred spoke. "The legend of the Coast Guard? Are you crazy?"

Dix answered, "I know it's a lot to handle, and we didn't want to believe it either, but it's clear he's the Caller. He does not have Coast Guard approval to use the jet he came in, I checked. Officially, he's on a two-week vacation. I need you guys to stay on the phone and let me know whenever you have something to report. Don't take Calhoun on yourselves, whatever you do."

Wilfred answered. "We'll watch for you, but if they start shooting, I'm not going to die just so you guys can catch Calhoun. We'll do what we can to help."

"That's all we ask. I'm guessing the dope is in the vehicle you saw go through the gate. Once they come out, they'll probably head to the airport. According to the lookouts there, Calhoun and his assistant are waiting on the tarmac next to one of the jets. Don't try to stop the SUV from making it to the plane."

Wilfred looked at Bubba. "Hold on a second. You want the dope to get through, right?"

"Yes, why?"

Wilfred looked at Bubba. "Get those dump trucks out of the way now, mon. We want them to get through."

Bubba stepped out of the car and made a few hand signals to the two men standing on the street. They jumped into their trucks and fired up the engines.

Bubba heard Dix laugh. "That was a great idea."

As the trucks moved away, the black SUV rolled slowly out of the tunnel entrance.

Bubba noticed the windows were down a few inches. He wasn't sure, but it looked like rifle barrels protruded slightly out of the two rear windows. As the vehicle reached the street, the driver slammed on the accelerator, and the vehicle lurched ahead. Bubba watched the SUV turn left and disappear. Then he lumbered back into his car.

Just as he fell into the passenger seat, Wilfred turned the key and spoke into the phone. "They just left the tunnel. The SUV looks loaded. The rear is sagging. And the windows were rolled down just far enough to get gun barrels through. The occupants appeared ready for a battle. They should be at the airport in a couple of minutes."

From the phone speaker came the response. "Okay. Tail them like you did before but try not to alert them to your presence. Keep the phone line open so we can communicate quickly."

Bubba shut his door, and they followed the black car. Once they reached the airport, Bubba and

Wilfred parked near a stand of trees and took a defensive position in case of a firefight. They laid out their extra magazines so they'd be available quickly if needed. Bubba glanced at the runway and was stunned. Two similar-looking G5 jets sat on the tarmac. The roar of their engines confirmed they were running. Through binoculars, Bubba noticed pilots in the cockpit of both planes. His mind raced to figure out what exactly Calhoun had up his sleeve.

"Holy shit!" he exclaimed as he pointed at the planes.

CHAPTER FORTY-SEVEN

Martin dumped the scooter he used to putt around the lodge property a few hundred yards from the airport and traveled the remaining distance rapidly on foot. He climbed a tree to get up on the ledge of an old building to gain a better vantage point. With his binoculars, he spotted Calhoun casually inhaling a cigar while he watched a black SUV pull between two jets. As the vehicle came to a stop, men jumped out and Martin watched as Calhoun began barking orders.

Martin couldn't hear what was being said and could not read lips.

Dix said this was going to be easy, he thought.

All he'd had to do was confirm if Calhoun showed up to the airport, watch him and try to remember everything he saw at the airport. If it seemed important, he was to call Petersen to let him know.

Suddenly, a massive explosion rocked him. Martin freaked out and saw a huge, fiery blaze mushrooming above the area where he thought the police storage shed was located. He certainly was not the man for this job. *Pull it together,* he thought.

Panning to his right, Martin spotted several Royal Bahamian Police Officers. They moved slowly toward a hangar near the tarmac. On the left, others in black jackets with "FBI" and "DEA" on the back also advanced toward the tarmac.

Martin guessed close to thirty law enforcement officials appeared to be circling the airport.

He looked back at the plume of smoke rising in the moonlight. His heart pounded in his chest as he thought about the situation in front of him. Thinking of Suzie helped him regain his composure. He turned back to get Calhoun in his sights. Now three men surrounded Calhoun, and it looked like they were arguing. *Oh shit, I need to call Petersen.*

He dialed Petersen, hoping for a quick answer.

* * * *

Dix and Petersen were at the command post a mile from the airport consulting with the Agents in Charge (AIC) of DEA, FBI, and the Royal Bahamian Police Commissioner.

Their phones squawked and the radios were a mess as everyone attempted to broadcast at the same time. The DEA boss listened for a moment. "Roger that." He turned to the detectives. "A firm perimeter is in place. You and the rest of our agents will be the arrest team. The locals will contain the scene and maintain the perimeter."

Dix paused for a moment. "Guys, I know this man. I understand criminals even better. These guys don't spend thirty years orchestrating lies and building empires to give up easily. From what I've heard, the guys in the DOG Unit with him are the best of the best as far as trained killers go, but I don't think they had any idea they were being used as pawns for Calhoun. We need to wait until the dope is unloaded and Calhoun gets into the plane with it before we strike."

As he finished, his phone rang.

"What's up, Martin?"

"Jesus, man. What are you guys doing? No one answers my calls. Where's Petersen, and what blew up?"

"Martin, you need to calm down. Just tell me what you see, and we'll figure this all out."

All this craziness on his little island had him freaked out. Martin was beside himself.

"Come on buddy, tell me what you see. Martin, you there?"

Martin regained his focus. "It looks like three guys have Calhoun surrounded. They look really pissed off. A black SUV showed up with the guys surrounding Calhoun, and there are two almost identical jets on the runway."

Dix hoped the DOG Unit knew what they were doing. Cornering a man like Calhoun could be catastrophic.

"Are they the same guys who arrived in the Denali?"

"Yes. I think so."

Dix covered the receiver on his phone and relayed the update to the bosses.

"What are they doing now?"

"They're screaming at each other. No one is backing off. There's another guy behind one of the jets. He sort of looks like a younger version of Calhoun. His rifle is trained on the men arguing with Calhoun."

"Okay, keep the line open. The wheels are falling off this one. When the shooting starts, stay low Martin."

Dix asked the OIC to order units to move in. Calhoun was close enough to the drugs and the evidence would be overwhelming. Dix couldn't think of a legitimate reason Calhoun had done what he had. He spoke into his phone. "Did you see the explosion?"

"Yeah. It was massive. Wait. A couple of guys are unloading the SUV now." Martin shouted. "Holy shit! Dix, I didn't see it before, but there's two of everything. Two black SUVs, two jets, and two groups of guys unloading the stuff from the SUVs into the jets. I can't tell who is who, man."

Dix shook his head. Son of a bitch, the confusion created by the explosion and the duplicate vehicle and jet would buy him time. He pleaded with the OIC. "We've got to go now."

Martin broke in. "Dix, they're done. Hold on…" the phone went dead.

* * * *

As Calhoun had slowly worked his way to the tarmac after leaving the storage facility and killing two local officers, he had noticed two local Bahamian men in an old car parked in a spot overlooking the airport. Their position would provide them a clear shot at him. He chuckled. *Couldn't have picked a better spot myself.*

His advantage was he was properly concealed and knew of their location. Once he arrived safely at the airport, he retrieved his sniper rifle. Now he eyed the two locals through his sniper rifle scope and thought about taking them out. He felt he should but had larger problems to deal with currently.

Calhoun hadn't anticipated the situation unraveling as it had and was forced to get to the runway immediately to meet with the DOG Unit. He knew the unit wouldn't let him down and calculated they'd be on the runway any second. The officers he spotted overlooking the area continued to nag at him. He determined they were too much of a threat. He calmly lined up each of them and killed them with a single round apiece.

He placed himself between the jets and the Yukon Denalis to ensure any other threats he might have missed wouldn't have a clear shot at him. His plan included jumping on the jet with the cocaine, with or without his son, and leaving the area for good.

Another part of the plan had failed, however. He was now face to face with Timms, Kemp, and Lester. They were pissed off and demanded more money.

Calhoun grimaced. "Where's Blanco?"

"We want a larger piece of the pie, Calhoun." Timms pressed.

Kemp scowled. "This shit just got real bad. We're going to need a whole lot more to disappear."

Calhoun replied smoothly, "Son, are you crazy? Who the hell are you... to challenge me? I made you, and I can take you out."

Kemp fired back. "More money or we don't finish unloading the dope and take it for ourselves." Calhoun didn't have an opportunity to reply.

Amidst the growing tension, a local officer pulled his gun from his thigh holster and inadvertently pulled the trigger. It was an accidental discharge. The bullet whizzed by the DOG team and struck the Yukon Denali they had just unloaded. The team and Calhoun took cover. Two of the DOG Unit men trained their rifles toward the area where they'd heard the shot originate while Timms pointed his weapon at Calhoun. Calhoun remained cool. He'd had guns pointed at him several times before in his life. "You kill me, you get no money. You take me in, you get no money. Put your gun away and finish the mission. I'll bump each of you to a million apiece when you help me off this island with the cocaine."

Timms smiled. "Deal."

* * * *

Over the radio, Dix ordered the arrest teams to split up and take on both jets.

As he finished the broadcast, the air thundered and lit up in a large plume of smoke, light, and debris. Everyone took cover.

Dix tossed his cell phone to Petersen. "Call Martin and find out what the hell just happened. Let's roll."

When they arrived on scene, Dix scanned the horizon for threats. Petersen motioned with his right thumb across his neck, letting Dix know Martin's line was dead. They couldn't look for him right then, the mission needed to move on without him.

They joined one of the teams converging on the tarmac while Dix noticed what looked like scraps of metal, tires, and other debris scattered in every direction. A large crater a few feet deep had scarred the runway.

He assumed it had been one of the SUVs. He feared the Coast Guard's first, and probably last, DOG Unit would be found amid the debris. *What a damn shame.*

Making a snap decision, he headed for the plane already facing to the east, which made it the most likely to take off first. Dix focused to locate Calhoun and the cocaine. After a few moments, he realized he could see no movement and hear no sounds of weapons being fired. Petersen looked at Dix and shrugged as if to say, "What the hell is going on?"

Dix wondered if he'd been tricked by Calhoun again, asking over the radio if anyone had eyes on Calhoun.

* * * *

Kemp turned to say something to Calhoun after loading the last duffel bag and was struck center mass by a sniper round.

The rest of the team returned fire at the shooter and tried to lock their sights on Calhoun as well.

Lester was clipped by a bullet in the shoulder, causing him to go down and Calhoun took a hit in the leg, and he buckled. The various threats demanding attention on the tarmac, coupled with Calhoun's position, made it difficult to get a clear shot at him.

Calhoun struggled to pull himself up and nodded to his son who was still in the cockpit of one of the jets. The sign told Junior to detonate the two bricks of dynamite secured beneath the large gas tank of the Denali the DOG Unit had used to deliver the cocaine.

The blast sent Calhoun back to the ground while debris and body parts rained from above. In an instant, the SUV was obliterated.

He fought to remain conscious. *Son of a bitch. My son finally came through.* An overwhelming sense of pride overcame him. It was short-lived. Shaking his head in an effort to stay awake, he noticed strike teams advancing in tight formations onto the tarmac. They broke into two lines to flank him and the jets.

He suddenly wasn't so certain he'd make it off the island with the cocaine. It also dawned on him that he didn't know for sure which jet actually contained the drugs. The confusion and confrontation with the remaining DOG members, and the assault from law enforcement on the airport had been too much for Calhoun to digest. He just wasn't sure of himself at that exact moment but assumed the dope was in the jet with his son. Moving as fast as his injured leg would take him, he tried to get on the plane with his son in the pilot's seat.

A paid-for-hire mercenary pilot, one used several times by Calhoun over the years, was making last minute preparations to taxi and take off in the other jet. As Calhoun had planned, one of the strike teams broke containment in an attempt to intercept the decoy jet. Calhoun chuckled and wondered how the advancing team intended to stop a jet while they were on foot.

The second team leader noticed the split in forces, and they moved forward as if to stop the second plane. Calhoun watched now as a few light Jeeps and trucks filled with snipers roared onto the tarmac. He had not prepared for this. Several loud shots echoed from a higher location as bits of asphalt exploded near the wheels of the jet.

Calhoun's leg throbbed. The wound was pretty bad, and he was functioning on pure adrenaline dragging his leg to make it to the plane.

The mercenary pilot changed course to avoid the bullets and tried to take off. Officers converged on foot and in vehicles. Law enforcement personnel surrounded the small airport and continued to add to the firefight.

As Calhoun pulled himself up into the cockpit, his son shot him a look. "You have to your promise that we'll keep the business going, with me in charge."

Calhoun was not in the mood to negotiate. He scowled. "You can take over the business. I'm done. Just get me the hell out of here." A loud explosion rocked the decoy jet. A fireball larger than he had ever seen rose from the tarmac, and he felt the intense heat and noticed the law enforcement people could not move forward. The decoy jet lay shattered and split in half from the explosion. It was engulfed in flames and blocking part of the runway.

"Dammit, we'll have to get around that plane," Junior shouted.

Calhoun looked at the kid. "Whatever it takes. These guys mean business. Get us out of here, now."

His son maneuvered the jet onto the main runway. He increased speed to get the jet off the ground. Dodging debris was proving to be a problem and it made it difficult getting up to speed.

Calhoun wore a grim smile. From the cockpit window, he noticed the blast from the other jet had disabled two law enforcement vehicles.

He counted several more men and one tiny Jeep converging on them. They were close enough for him to read their jackets. He saw several federal agencies were involved, which caused him a great deal of concern. Their involvement meant they had concrete evidence against him. He had no way of knowing how they'd obtained it.

Nevertheless, he was confident they were mere yards from taking to the air. If they didn't make it, he'd already decided he wouldn't go to prison. He'd commit suicide first. He watched the driver of the utility vehicle miscalculate how much room he needed to negotiate the new crater in the runway. The right front wheel caught the lip causing the Jeep to roll. Bodies flew. *Oh well, just more collateral damage,* thought Calhoun.

Calhoun watched as his son finished the short taxi and turned the nose of the jet toward freedom. The plane was now taking rounds from advancing law enforcement. The seats and other material within the plane exploded as bullets ripped through the fuselage. Calhoun wondered if the plane would hold together even if they could get it airborne.

The runway was littered with debris, but his son found enough room to maneuver the jet. Continual smaller explosions from flash bangs and hand grenades lobbed at the fleeing jet filled the area.

All the guys I hired for this operation were imbeciles. None of them could be trusted. Calhoun began to think he'd have to put a bullet in his own head. It was his fault for trusting others to carry out his plans.

* * * *

As the intensity of the flames from the burning jet dissipated, the first strike team converged on it with the airport's lone fire truck. At best, the scene could have been described as utter pandemonium.

Petersen focused on the second jet and pointed. "I see two men, one looks like Calhoun and one who looks like that assistant he brought. They're both in the cockpit."

Dix ran in the general direction of the occupied jet and noticed a small Jeep barreling toward him to his right. Petersen ran close behind.

As the vehicle skidded to a stop in front of them, Dix and Petersen jumped in.

Dix grinned at Roger, who was seated in the driver's seat. "Where the heck did you get this thing?"

"Snagged it near a gift shop after I got my bearings back.

Now, let's get this bastard."

Dix had feared Roger might have been killed in the earlier blast at the storage facility and was happy to see him alive.

More fire trucks from the city and ambulances arrived at the airport. Nevertheless, the few local Bahamian resources were quickly depleted.

Dix turned to Roger. "Keep the jet from getting into the air. Pull in front of it. Do whatever you have to do, but that bird isn't flying today."

Roger stepped on the accelerator, and the Jeep's engine roared to life. Dix asked Petersen if he had a phone. Petersen tossed his to Dix, and he speed dialed Wilfred, who picked up on the first ring.

"Where's Bubba?"

"Working on a Plan B," Wilfred yelled. His excitement came through in his voice.

Dix wasn't sure what Plan B was. He hoped whatever it was, it would happen soon.

"Wilfred, whatever you guys came up with, act now! We need the jet disabled. Petersen, Roger, and I are on the tarmac headed right for it." A loud boom caused Dix to drop the phone. He frantically grabbed for it as it bounced on the floorboard of the Jeep. "We're in the small Jeep headed right at the jet. We may not be able to keep the plane from taking off but we're gonna try."

"Here comes Bubba. He's in a huge Peterbilt Truck." The line went dead.

Roger spotted the crater created when the DOG SUV had blown up. He tried to miss it, but the front tire caught as he was checking out the dump truck. The Jeep rolled one time and ended right side up, but all three occupants were ejected.

Roger's left leg had a nasty gash, and he was losing a lot of blood. He was unconscious but still breathing. Dix checked himself and realized he'd probably broken his left arm. The pain in his chest indicated some broken ribs as well. He could taste blood in his mouth. He looked for his partner. Petersen was walking off to his left and appeared relatively unscathed. In the distance behind Petersen, Dix spotted two Stingray Coast Guard helicopters heading toward them. The excitement was getting out of hand.

Petersen looked at Dix and started to run his way. Dix yelled "Are you all right?"

"I feel fine. I must be the luckiest son of a bitch in the world right now. You okay?"

"A couple broken bones, but nothing serious. Roger's hurt bad."

Petersen assessed the situation. "We need to get him out of here ASAP or he could bleed out."

Dix pointed at the Jeep. "You think it's operational?"

"Only one way to find out."

"Get Roger in it, and get him to the hospital."

"Bill, you're hurt. He's hurt. Get in the damn Jeep so I can take you both to the hospital."

Dix shook his head. He had a score to settle. "I outrank you and order you to get that man to the hospital."

The jet had positioned itself at the end of the runway and began to accelerate for takeoff.

A few DEA and FBI agents fired rounds at the wheels. Others screamed on their radios for more backup. Calhoun fired suppression rounds from a window already shattered from law enforcement fire.

Dix was feeling weak and his vision had begun to blur. He wanted to take Calhoun into custody in person but knew his body wouldn't allow it. *Not this time.*

An international criminal and political catastrophe were unfolding right in front of him, and he was unable to stop it. He'd experienced defeat before, but this was personal.

The Coast Guard helicopters had arrived overhead and tried to prevent the plane from taking off by getting low. Dix thought he saw a bright light and what he thought was a smile on Petersen's face as he fell to the ground. Then he lost consciousness.

CHAPTER FORTY-EIGHT

Dix opened his eyes and instantly knew where he was. The sounds, smells, and bed always felt the same. He glanced around the hospital room and spotted balloons and flowers. A stack of envelopes sat on the bedside table… get well cards. To his right, Roger sat, propped up with several pillows watching the television.

"I'm glad to see you made it, Roger. You didn't look so good out there on the runway." Dix grinned.

Roger chuckled and then grimaced. "Look who's talking. I'm quite well. They saved my leg, but I'll be here for a while. We can spend some quality time together."

Dix started to laugh but felt a sharp pain in his side. His left arm was immobilized in a cast, and his vision was still a little blurred. He had the mother of all headaches. But he was alive and stable. He knew he'd eventually walk away from yet another serious injury. *Well, I managed to make it through another battle.*

He was thankful to be alive, but the positive thoughts didn't last very long. He assumed Calhoun had slipped away or was dead. All the planning and cooperation from so many agencies and they couldn't snare one guy. *What a joke. A very bad one.*

Not really wanting to ask, but knowing he had to, he said, "Roger, what happened to that bastard, Calhoun?"

Roger wrinkled his forehead. "I haven't heard a word. When they brought me in, I was out cold just like you. I came out of surgery before you, but the sedatives and painkillers they used were pretty strong. Petersen's been here checking on you almost every hour. He just left to get a bite to eat. I'm sure he'll know."

Dix realized what a great partner Petersen was. He decided to take it a little easier on him from now on. He felt some remorse about teasing him about his ex-wife. *Steve deserves to be happy.*

Twenty minutes passed, and Petersen still hadn't returned. Dix grew anxious. He needed to know what had happened at the airport. If it hadn't been for the cast on his left arm and all the tubes and wires hooked up to him, he'd have left to track Petersen down himself.

Then he realized the story would surely be on the television.

He looked at his roommate. "Hey, can you change the channel to the local news?"

"This silly television only gets *The Price is Right* and *Golden Girls*. Sorry, mon."

"Great. I'm stuck on an island with two TV channels. This is killing me. Which one of these buttons will bring a nurse?"

"Hit the red one, but before you do, I'll clue you in. The lady who'll show up isn't pleasant, just so you know." Roger grinned.

Dix hit the button about ten times anyway. He dared some nurse to give him any problems right now. He was in pain and wanted questions answered.

The door to their room opened. Petersen strolled in with a grin on his face. He walked directly to Dix's bed.

"Hey pal, how are you?"

"Man, I'm glad to see you. I assume you got me and Roger here. I owe you my life now, but don't let it go to your head."

Petersen chuckled. "Yep, judging by that attitude, you're closer to a full recovery already."

"All kidding aside, Steve, thank you for taking care of me and Roger. I'm sorry I mess with you so much."

Petersen shrugged. "You'd have done the same for us. I don't like sentimental crap. I prefer grumpy

Bill Dix. How come you haven't asked me what finally happened on the tarmac?"

"I was getting to that, but I'd better lie down. I feel a little light headed. While I suffer, could you fill me in?"

Petersen pulled up a chair close beside the bed. "I dragged you and Roger in the Jeep. It wasn't easy, and I wasn't in the best of shape either. But I managed. As I raced toward the closest hospital, Calhoun's jet was about to take off. The runway was filled with debris, but it looked like they might make it."

Petersen grabbed the water bottle on the table, poured himself a glass and drank.

Dix grimaced. "Hey, buddy, that's mine."

Petersen just grinned. "Glad you're here to drink it."

Dix had a sheepish grin on his face. "Hurry up and get on with the story."

"Well, I turned my attention toward driving you two to safety. I figured the bastards were gone. I made it just outside the gates to the airport when I heard a thunderous crash. The hair on the back of my neck literally stood up. You started screaming something about getting the prick bastard, and rambling about Roger losing blood."

Dix nodded impatiently.

"Anyway, I looked back and a huge Peterbilt truck had smashed into the rear of the plane. A white cloud of cocaine dust blew through the air. I saw Bubba and Wilfred pull each other from the wreckage. The local officers and Feds converged on the plane. They were trying to stabilize the scene before the truck and jet ignited."

"Oh, man, that must have been crazy. How many lives were lost?"

"Two local cops were found dead. Turns out they were under investigation by the DEA and FBI for drug trafficking. They think Calhoun had killed them on his way to the airport. No one else died, but plenty were injured."

Roger asked, "How are Bubba and Wilfred?"

Petersen grinned. "As they got out of the Peterbilt, Calhoun, who somehow managed to survive the collision, started firing on them. Calhoun shot Bubba in the leg, which really pissed him off. Wilfred fired back and…"

Dix interrupted. "Don't tell me, Wilfred killed Calhoun?"

Petersen replied. "Nope. He was flanking Calhoun and shot him right in the butt."

Dix laughed. "Are you kidding me? So he's here?"

Petersen held up his hand. "That's not the end of the story. Witnesses said it looked like Calhoun's pilot tried to help him, but they were arguing over something. Calhoun baited the guy to come closer and shot him. The Feds think the pilot might have been related to Calhoun because of his striking resemblance. DNA may confirm it. No one knew anything about him." Petersen wore a broad smile.

Dix raised an eyebrow. "Are you making this stuff up?"

"I know it sounds surreal, but it's the truth according to a contact at the Coast Guard working with DEA and FBI. They think maybe the guy was Calhoun's son, and he was trying to take over the family business. They believe this was Calhoun's last deal, and he was going to quit for good. Just poof, disappear."

Dix shook his head in disbelief.

Roger asked, "Where the heck is Martin?"

Petersen shot Dix a look of concern. Dix looked sick to his stomach as though he assumed the worst had happened to Martin.

"No thanks to you, he got too close to the runway and the explosion knocked him unconscious."

Dix felt terrible and stared out the hospital window while shaking his head.

"Relax buddy, he was asleep during the whole takedown."

Dix stopped shaking his head but continued to look out the window. "Where's he now?"

"With his wonderful wife. She's taking great care of him."

Dix looked back at Petersen. "Man, he could have been killed. I guess I was so desperate to catch Calhoun and made a bad call."

Petersen shrugged, "Oh, get over it. By the way, your wife is here when you're ready to see her."

Then Petersen confirmed that Calhoun was in custody, and he told Dix how Calhoun had tried to kill himself once already. "When that didn't work, Calhoun told the Feds he could lead them to someone much more dangerous. The DEA guy told Calhoun that Blanco, the only surviving member of the DOG team, was talking. Calhoun was furious and now he's desperate. Blanco's supposed to receive a medal for his efforts to try to stop Calhoun."

Dix looked out the window again, happy to be alive. He turned back to Petersen. "So, what's next?"

Petersen had disappeared and in his place he saw an angel, his beautiful wife. She raced to his side in tears. *This is going to hurt like hell, but I'm going to love every second of it.*

THE END

GRAY GHOST

(Bill Dix Detective Series)

By

C.L. Swinney

Made in the USA
Lexington, KY
02 July 2017